THE BEAST

CLAN ROSS OF THE HEBRIDES

HILDIE McQUEEN

USA TODAY BESTSELLING AUTHOR

Pink Door Publishing

ISBN: 978-1-939356-91-8

Also By Hildie McQueen

CLAN ROSS OF THE HEBRIDES

This fictional story takes place at the beginning of the 17th century in the Scottish Hebrides, isles off the Isle of Skye's western coasts.

In the 1500s, lordship over the Hebrides collapsed and the power was given to clan chiefs. The MacNeil, in Barra, The Macdonald (Clanranald), in South Uist, The Uisdein, in North Uist and the MacLeod, the isles of Harris and Lewis.

For this series, I have moved the clans around a bit to help the story work better. The clans' locations in my books are as follows. The MacNeil will remain in Barra, The Macdonald (Clanranald) is moved to North Uist, The Uisdein resides in Benbecula, and the MacLeod remains in the Isles of Harris and Lewis. My fictional clan, Clan Ross, will laird over South Uist.

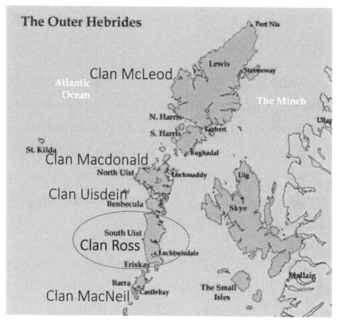

Clan Ross of the Hebrides Map

After the death of their father, Laird Calum Ross, the Ross siblings learn of the atrocities he committed against the clan. They must work hard to regain the people's trust and begin anew.

Each of the seven Ross siblings come to terms with their new roles as leaders responsible for hundreds of families.

One by one, they will find their calling, their place, and hopefully a love for all time.

How can such a hauntingly beautiful man hold so much ugliness within?

Duncan Ross's inner scars are even more horrifying than the visible ones. Unable to control his rages, he hides himself away from his close-knit family. He has long accepted the painful truth that he will never have a wife or a family of his own. When a beautiful woman tells her family they are courting, he is forced to make an agonizing decision that will break her heart and shatter his lonely soul.

As the pampered daughter of a powerful laird, Beatrice Macdonald is rarely taken seriously. When her sister marries Laird Ross, she fights to remain at Keep Ross to ensure her sister is well treated. In order to make her case, Beatrice lies and tells her mother that Duncan Ross is courting her for marriage. However, the more she gets to know the reclusive man and his secrets, the more she realizes that she picked the wrong Ross brother for the ruse.

CHAPTER ONE

North Uist Sea
Late Summer 1601

THE WIND BLEW hard, tossing the bìrlinn sideways and Duncan Ross was glad he was not prone to sea sickness. The bìrlinn rose and fell, as a tall wave hit, and the crew scrambled to adjust the sails.

His clothing soaked through, Duncan clung to a large mast while yanking at ropes, attempting with the other men to keep some sort of control over the boat.

"Bloody hell," his brother Stuart stared out to the waters, as if he could pacify the wind with but a glare. "Hopefully we will not drown today."

Duncan pointed toward the west. "I see the North Uist shore now. We should arrive unscathed."

"And sopping wet," Stuart grumbled. "I am not amused."

As of late, his brother had been complaining non-stop, which was why their eldest brother, Laird Ross, had insisted he go with Duncan to visit the Macdonald on North Uist. His brother's hazel gaze roamed over the waves, dark hair flying about his head making him look like an angry pirate. A pirate that hated being on water.

Normally the travel by bìrlinn from South Uist took an entire day, if leaving first thing in the morning, they would usually arrive by late evening. Not this day. Despite leaving early in the morning, it was now pitch black and well into the night.

They'd have to sleep in the birlinn and await daylight to make their way to Keep Macdonald. It would be an uncomfortable night, to say the least. They would have to change into dry clothes and make a fire to dry the ones they currently wore.

Upon arriving ashore, they were met by guardsmen who informed Duncan they were expected. Duncan was relieved to see that the Macdonald men had a huge bonfire going, along with warmed blankets and tents erected for them to sleep in.

Grateful for the kindness, Duncan and his crew hurried to undress and drape the wet clothing near the fire to dry. Thankfully, he'd packed his plaid, so he wrapped himself in the dry garment and joined the others for a simple meal of roasted meat and bread, which tasted pleasing to his empty stomach.

A young man with dark brown hair and just as dark eyes, neared and sat next to Duncan. "I am Padraig Macdonald, second son of Laird Macdonald," he said by way of introduction.

His gaze moved from Duncan to Stuart. "I remember ye," he said to Stuart. "It has not been too long since we last saw each other."

Stuart nodded. "Aye, the last time our mothers met." He motioned to Duncan. "My brother, Duncan. He is second born as well."

"How does yer father fare?" Duncan asked, knowing the Macdonald had been stricken by a crippling affliction.

"He is well," Padraig said with a smile. "His lack of proper mobility does not prevent him from keeping my brother, Evander, and I in line."

It was evident the young warrior loved his father deeply and Duncan found it hard to understand. His father had been one of the cruelest people he'd ever known, which was stating something as he'd encountered many a horrible person.

"I look forward to our meeting tomorrow," Duncan added.

Padraig got to his feet and glared around the group, seeming to realize something. "Where the hell is my sister? Did something happen to her? Why is she not here?" He shot out the questions, not waiting for a reply.

Stuart looked to Duncan. "Did we forget Miss Beatrice?"

"Nay," Duncan replied. "Yer sister refused to come with us. She sent a letter to yer mother asking permission to remain longer."

Padraig blew out a breath, not seeming happy at all. "Impetuous as always. She should have been brought by force."

When neither Ross said anything, Padraig continued, "My parents will be very disappointed in Beatrice not returning. She has already extended her stay once."

Unsure what to say, Duncan chose to not comment. Stuart, however, was not so inclined.

"It seems she and Isobel are very close. I believe they are having a hard time accepting that they will be separated now. Miss Beatrice has also grown attached to our sister, Ella, as well."

With a chuckle, Padraig shook his head. "My sisters are both opposites and very much alike. Isobel tends to act the protector; however, it is Beatrice who has the protective nature of a wild beast when their young are threatened."

Duncan pictured the diminutive woman and could not imagine her furious. She was friendly and from the very short time he'd been around her, kind. Unlike most, who gave him wide berth, Beatrice had conversed with him in what he could only describe as a personal manner usually only shown by his family.

Admittedly, he was part of her circle now, being her sister was married to his brother, Darach. It was still strange to him that she'd not acted the least bit put off by him, her friendliness had caught him by surprise.

He'd happened upon her in his family parlor, and she'd struck up a conversation. Not a long one, mostly asking that he deliver a letter. She'd also commented on the fact his eyes were two colors and that her brother Evander also had two different colored eyes.

The most curious thing had been when she'd placed a hand on his forearm. The intimacy of the touch nearly had him demand she remove her hand immediately. That strong had been his reaction to her touch.

MORNING CAME TOO soon. Duncan was roused early by the sounds of the men preparing to continue to the Macdonald keep. He'd slept soundly, tired after two days of preparing for the trip and the unfriendly seas that greeted them.

Once dressed, he helped take down the tents and packed his sack onto a cart that had been brought by the Macdonald's.

Everyone then mounted horses that had also been brought and they rode for half a day to Keep Macdonald.

Feeling well-rested, he took time to take in the surroundings of North Uist. He'd been on the shore several times but had not come so far inland. There had never been a need for it as most of his dealings had been with ship captains, who remained on the shorelines.

Although still a bit away, the Macdonald keep was visible. The quaint keep was built on high ground, constructed on a hill that was next to a large loch.

The views from the front of the home would allow for the inhabitants to see anyone heading their way. What struck him as interesting was that the entire keep, including the surrounding wall, was whitewashed.

He looked to Stuart. "Why would anyone do that to a building? It stands out for miles."

Stuart nodded. "Aye, I remember thinking the same when I first visited. The stones found on this isle are of that color, is what was explained to me. I am told the material is very resilient."

Upon arriving, the gates were already open, so they followed Padraig through them.

They were ushered through the outer courtyard where they dismounted and walked into the inner courtyard, which again was different, Keep Ross only had one courtyard. Then again, the Macdonald's army was not as large as theirs and they needed the additional protection.

Who Duncan figured to be the eldest brother, Evander Macdonald, and Lady Macdonald greeted them at the door. The woman looked past him to the younger son. Her expression became one of alarm. Eyes widened she searched the group. "Where is Beatrice?"

Lady Aileen Macdonald had reddish-brown hair and

bright green eyes. Despite wisps of silver hair appearing at her temples, she remained an attractive woman.

"I will explain once we go inside," Padraig said with a half-smile. "Ye're going to be cross."

The woman's eyes went to Duncan, they narrowed, but she nodded silently.

"Welcome," Evander said taking a step forward. "I am Evander Macdonald. I do not believe to have met ye. I have met all of yer brothers. I trust yer travel went well. With the strong winds, we wondered if ye would be waylaid."

"We almost were," Duncan said. "Thank ye for sending the men to give us a dry, warm place to sleep. It was much appreciated by my men and myself."

Instantly Duncan noticed that Evander's eyes, like his, were of two different colors. Unlike his brown and hazel, Evander's were brown and blue.

It was interesting, that despite having the feature himself it struck him as odd. For an instant, they locked gazes before looking away. The man was tall, though not quite as tall as him. But then very few men were a head above six feet. Evander had broad shoulders and the same auburn hair color as his mother's.

"My father awaits ye." Evander motioned for them to walk inside and they made their way into a great hall where a table was set with food and drink.

Laird Macdonald stood upon seeing them. By the grunts and wobbly motions, it was obvious it took effort. Although not an old man, the affliction that ailed him made him appear older. However, his sharp blue gaze reminded one of his authority.

The laird looked to him and Stuart. "It is always easy to recognize a Ross. Tall and well built," he stated. "Welcome."

Once the greetings were completed, they sat at a long table that had been prepared for them. Servants hurried to fill the tankards with sweet-smelling ale and bowls of spiced meat and potatoes were placed in front of them. Bread, cheese, and thinly sliced boar meat on wooden boards, as well as a platter piled high with fruit tarts, rounded out the meal offerings.

Before delving into the food that made his mouth water, Duncan handed the letter from Beatrice to Lady Macdonald.

"Yer daughter would not travel back with us. She stated her wish to spend more time with her sister."

Lady Macdonald slipped the letter onto her lap. "I will be forced to fetch her myself. I am certainly cross," she gave Padraig a pointed look. "Ye must come with me when I go."

"Ye cannot go until after the MacLeod visit," the laird said patiently. "Lady MacLeod will be expecting to spend time with ye."

When the laird turned to Duncan, Lady Macdonald made a face. It seemed she was not as enthused about the MacLeod visit as her husband.

"As ye and yer brother are no doubt aware, we have a close alliance with the MacLeods. There's a friendship between myself and the MacLeod," Laird Macdonald informed them.

Duncan nodded. "We are very much aware. Now that our clans are to be allies, we hope to also gain the trust of the MacLeod."

"Well said young man," the Macdonald stated. "Trust must exist for a true alliance to form. The marriage between our clans is a formality, but in truth, I am hopeful that we will gain a deeper friendship. I know it will make both my wife and yer mother very happy."

Lady Macdonald nodded. "Indeed, it would. I do apologize for my daughter over-extending the boundaries of propriety when it comes to prolonging her visit, yet again."

"My brother asked that we inform ye that she is more than welcome. It makes Isobel happy for her sister to remain and it is not an encumbrance in the least," Stuart assured Lady Macdonald.

The woman looked less than convinced. "I cannot imagine what reason she gives me."

Once the meal was over, Duncan and his brother were shown their chambers. They would only remain two nights and from there they were to meet with the sea captain before making their way back to South Uist.

Sometime later, Stuart walked into Duncan's bedchamber. "What do ye think? If we form a strong alliance between the three clans, we are guaranteeing peace for our people."

His brother held out a glass with what Duncan assumed was whisky. It tasted earthy and rich. Duncan lifted the drink and studied it. "We must ask for some of this to take back. It is very good."

"Which is why I brought it. Padraig says they purchase it from a local man who has spent years perfecting it."

The amber liquid slid down his throat making a warming trail down to his stomach. "And so, we will purchase some to take back." He went to the window and peered down at the inner courtyard. People meandered about, preparing for the second part of the day.

Servants fed chickens, while young men tended to goats in

a corral. There were several guardsmen walking atop the outer courtyard walkway, their heads turning every so often to take in what happened down below them.

It wasn't too different than Keep Ross; however, there seemed to be a peace about the place. A sense of quiet and something Duncan couldn't quite put his finger on. "I do not think I could live here."

Stuart joined him at the window. "I'd miss the smell of the sea. No view of the waves and the closest mountain is barely visible."

"I suppose that is it." He wasn't convinced. Something about the place made him uneasy, which made no sense. The people were friendly and there was no reason for him not to trust. It wasn't the Macdonald's he decided. It was what the building and the surroundings reminded him of a place he fought to forget but was forever branded into his mind and body.

He'd once been held captive off the coast of Spain. Whenever he was allowed on the ship's deck, he'd stared at the whitewashed buildings that dotted the landscape. How he'd loathed the view of promise that would never come to be.

LAST MEAL WAS served and again the fare was beyond reproach. Duncan ate his fill unable to keep from eating more than he should.

"Lady Macdonald, I must compliment yer cook. The meal is delicious," Stuart, ever the diplomat told the hostess, who beamed with pride.

"Her name is Willa; she is actually quite young. However, her cooking is beyond reproach and the reason why we are visited again and again by people hoping to taste what she serves."

The woman studied Duncan for a long moment. "My daughter writes and informs me that she had occasion to spend time with ye."

Stuart along with Evander and Padraig all turned to him with curious expressions.

"Aye, we spoke in the parlor once. She noted that Evander and I have the same trait. Eyes of two different colors."

"Oh, my goodness," Lady Macdonald leaned forward studying his face. "Ye do." She whirled to her son. "Evander, did ye notice?"

"I did Mother," her son replied giving Duncan a knowing look.

Lady Macdonald studied them each again. "Evander's eyes are blue and brown, where yers are the Ross hazel in yer left eye and brown in the right. How delightful," she exclaimed.

He and Evander looked at one another for a split second, a sort of bonding over their trait forming.

The Macdonald looked from his son to Duncan. "A Mac-Neil trait I believe."

"Aye, it is," Lady Macdonald said with a wide smile. "My own father had two different colored eyes. One brown and one hazel, like yers, Duncan."

"I have met my grandfather and it was strange to see someone else who had the same eyes as me," Evander said. "Now ye are the second person."

Duncan didn't like being looked at so closely. When people studied a person overly long, sometimes they noted the hidden things.

Thankfully, just then musicians entered to entertain, and everyone returned to their meals.

DUNCAN RUSHED TO his room as soon as he could without seeming rude. He was not comfortable with so many people he didn't know, and the music didn't help settle him at all. As a matter of fact, most times he found it to be an annoyance.

He paced the bedchamber as familiar aches began. The torment was not only physical, but it was mental as well. His mind would go to dark places and there was little he could do to stop it. This was a most inconvenient time as the episodes of despondency would sometimes last two or three days. At home, he'd work until too tired to move or he'd lock himself in his room and keep away from people. Here neither option was a possibility.

"Not now," he gritted the words out loud through a clenched jaw.

Knocks on the door made him want to scream for the person to go away. If it were not that he was somewhere unfamiliar, he would have.

"Come in."

Lady Macdonald appeared holding a tray with two cups upon it. "Herbs for yer head. Yer brother told me ye suffer from headaches. I do not wish to disturb ye but would like a word in private before ye retire."

Forcing himself to settle, he motioned to a chair and lowered to the one next to it. He picked up the cup feeling out of sorts holding the delicate item in his large, calloused hands.

The liquid was sweet and tasted of spices, he'd never had before. "What is this?"

"It is a spice called cinnamon that I purchased from one of the ships that stopped here for a while after suffering some damage."

Duncan drank it down, enjoying how the fragrance combined with the boiled herb did indeed help him settle.

"Here drink mine as well," Lady Macdonald pushed her full cup into his hands.

He drank, but this time slower. "What did ye wish to speak with me of Lady Macdonald?"

"Beatrice's letter. I did not wish to say more in front of my husband and sons. She claims ye have expressed a desire to court."

"Court?" Duncan looked into the cup wondering if he could ask for more. It was delicious and it would give him time to consider how to reply. "I am not sure what ye mean."

Lady Macdonald chuckled. "Ye have a headache and I am sure this is not the most appropriate time to speak of such things. However, since ye leave soon, I find there is no other time."

"Aye, of course," Duncan replied focusing on the woman. "What exactly did yer daughter write that concerns me?"

With a look of confusion, Lady Macdonald pulled the letter from the hidden pocket within her dress folds. "She states that ye have expressed a desire to court her for marriage and that is why she wishes to remain there longer."

Duncan waited for a moment hoping to come up with a suitable response. He didn't wish to tell Lady Macdonald that her daughter lied. Could it be he'd said something that would have led the lass to think he was courting her?

"When we spoke, we did not come to any avowal," he

finally said.

"But ye do wish to court her? Or should I assume that my daughter has been otherwise compromised?"

His eyes rounded. "Not at all. We have not been alone, except for once, and only briefly."

"I see." Lady Macdonald lifted a brow. "Ye have not replied to my first question."

Despite his lack of being part of any courting ritual in his life, Duncan knew enough about mothers to keep from angering Lady Macdonald in any fashion.

"I find Miss Beatrice to be exquisite. In truth, I do not believe to have ever met a woman as beautiful. It would be an honor to court her."

Duncan was satisfied he'd replied correctly without compromising himself. It seemed Lady Macdonald was not as happy with his reply. Her eyes narrowed and she studied him for a beat longer than comfortable.

"We shall discuss this further upon my visit to South Uist. It will be at least a sennight until I arrive, hopefully not more. I must wait until after the MacLeod's visit. Hopefully, they will not extend their stay past two or three days."

She took the empty cup from his hand and the other one and placed them back on the tray. "I will ensure to pack some of this cinnamon for ye to take. Let yer cook know it must boil in the water until the aroma rises."

When the woman walked out, Duncan was too preoccupied with what Beatrice had written that he didn't notice the episode that had threatened was gone.

Why would the lass write such a thing? If anything, he was the one she'd spoken to least of all his brothers. From what

Stuart had said, she'd spent a great deal of time with Gideon.

He considered their conversation in the parlor. She'd held a journal and had prepared quill and paper to write to her mother about her desire to remain at Keep Ross longer.

Everyone knew the reason. Isobel, her sister and Darach, his brother, were going through a rough time. Isobel was not in good spirits and Beatrice wished to be there to comfort her sister. It was the second time she'd extended her visit, which was good news for both Isobel and Duncan's sister, Ella, who'd become very close to Beatrice.

Obviously, Lady Macdonald had been misled to think he was to court Beatrice.

Duncan sighed and looked around the bedchamber. The Macdonalds did not spare expense in furnishings. Nor in any other manner from what he'd seen. The men were dressed in fine fabrics and Beatrice's dress, the day he'd spoken to her, had been exquisite.

They were wealthy and had no need for an alliance, other than to ensure future peace. It would be in his clan's interest to remain closely bonded with this clan. However, he was not the right man to marry the beautiful Beatrice.

Never once, since his escape from capture, had he ever considered courting a woman with the intent to marry.

As a matter of fact, he didn't allow himself to dream of a normal life, with a wife and bairns. That was not to be his reality.

Courtship to a laird's daughter was an impossibility. One did not court such a woman unless with the intention of marriage. And the one thing Duncan was sure about was that he would never marry.

CHAPTER TWO

Dún Láidir, Keep Ross, South Uist

Beatrice Macdonald paced the parlor impatient to know what would happen upon her mother opening the letter she'd sent. It had been four days since Duncan and Stuart had gone to North Uist and they were expected to return this day. The next day at the latest.

If her mother returned with them, she wasn't sure what would happen. Of course, she'd immediately inform her that she'd not been truthful in stating that Duncan was courting her. No sooner had he left with the letter than she'd realized what a dreadful mistake she'd made.

What if her brother read it and demanded Duncan marry her immediately? Or if her mother returned with him and insisted there be a wedding? Goodness, the things she got herself into by being so impetuous.

"I have been searching for ye everywhere," Ella Ross said as she walked in and came to stand next to Beatrice. "Should have known ye would be here, as much as ye like the view from these windows." Ella reminded her so much of her brothers with dark brown hair and hazel eyes. She was tall for a woman, but unlike the muscular Ross men, she was curvy.

"How can ye not?" Beatrice replied with a smile. "The waves are mesmerizing."

"Indeed," Ella said following her line of sight to the darkening waters as the sun had recently set. "I do love it. However, I am not here to speak of the view, but to make plans for our traveling to the village tomorrow."

"Tomorrow?"

Ella gave her a quizzical look. "There is to be a festival at the village square, and Gideon has agreed to escort us."

"That is wonderful," Beatrice replied with as much enthusiasm as she could muster. "It will be a distraction from worry. I am so very anxious to hear what Mother's reply will be. I know she will be displeased at me for extending my visit."

"Bah!" Ella exclaimed with a wave of her hand. "I am sure she will be glad to come to fetch ye as she and Mother enjoy spending time together."

"If she comes right away, yer mother is gone. The only ones here are ye and I."

Laird Darach Ross, Beatrice's sister Isobel, and Lady Mariel Ross had all gone to the Isle of Barra to visit Clan MacNeil. They were not expected to return for at least a sennight, perhaps longer.

It was best to make the most out of her time there Beatrice considered. "Tomorrow we go to the village and we stay as long as we wish because if Mother arrives, my freedom may well be over."

"Ye fret too much. I am sure yer mother will not mind traveling here. Duncan and Stuart return soon and once they do, ye will see that all is well."

Her friend studied her for a moment and then smiled. "I bid ye a good night."

Once Ella left, Beatrice settled into a comfortable chair and continued her perusal of the darkening view. Her friend was right. Other than her mother possibly being annoyed with her; she'd spend a few days there and then she and her mother would return to North Uist together.

The thought of returning home made her sad. Not only would Isobel not be there, but she'd be without her new friend Ella.

Her acquaintances back in North Uist would provide a good distraction. Although in fairness, they did little more than gather for tea, needlework, and walks.

For some reason life at Keep Ross was much more entertaining. There were the morning visits from villagers, a parade of peddlers, the siblings' interactions at dinnertime. They squabbled and always debated different topics over last meal.

In comparison, her home life was more what she would describe as peaceful. Her brothers and father kept from discussing anything of importance at the table. Usually, it was her mother who carried the conversation, which centered on what needed to be done around the keep.

At Keep Ross, the views of the sea from almost every window were enchanting. The beauty of it never waning. Beatrice could spend hours just looking out at the never-ending ebb and flow of the waves.

ONCE IN BED, Beatrice looked up at the ceiling and considered what would happen if her mother approached Duncan about her letter. The poor man would be caught by surprise and would probably give away the fact he had no intention of courting her. Not only that, but he would probably inform her mother it was a lie as well.

Because Duncan Ross did not live at the keep, she'd not gotten to know him well. The conversation they had in the parlor prior to him leaving had been their first and only one. He'd come offering to take her back home since he was traveling to North Uist.

It had been after that conversation and a strange feeling she got from speaking with him that made her choose him as being the one courting her.

At the time, it had made sense. Her mother would come to fetch her and would probably not run into him since he lived elsewhere. The plan had merit, except for that she'd not considered that he'd be delivering the message.

Poor Duncan, he did not deserve for her to put him in such a spot. He was already a quiet man, surely her mother's questioning would put him ill at ease.

There was an ambiguity about him. Even when his siblings referred to him, it was as if they held back a secret, something that they kept hidden within the family.

Despite his large size, muscular build, and elusiveness, she'd found herself drawn to him. It could be because he had two different colored eyes like her brother, Evander; or that despite his quiet nature, he seemed kind. Admittedly with his dark brown hair he kept pulled back and tied with a strap and the dark shadowing on his strong jaw, he was particularly handsome. He had a dangerous allure that attracted Beatrice.

So much about Duncan Ross made her curious to find out more. Perhaps she'd ask Ella questions during their ride to the village the following day.

After all, she expected there would be a conversation between her and Duncan upon his return. She would be seeking him out to apologize for misleading her mother and implicating him in her schemes.

A shiver went through her at the thought of the huge man becoming angry. What would his reaction be?

She closed her eyes and the image of his face appeared. He was handsome, his mannerisms so measured it was as if he fought for control of each movement and word he spoke. Beatrice turned to her side and listened to the sounds of the ocean until it seemed to permeate everything in the bedchamber.

THE NEXT MORNING, first meal was a hurried affair as Beatrice and Ella were anxious to prepare for their day and head to the festival.

Having ordered a carriage be prepared, all that was left for them to do was to fetch their shawls and ensure Gideon was ready to escort them.

"Where is my brother?" Ella exclaimed with an annoyed huff. "I hope not to have to wake him."

Beatrice studied her friend. They decided to wear serviceable gowns, so they'd not stand out too much. Ella wore a dark brown dress, her vest just a shade lighter and her wavy hair had been brushed back and braided. A single braid hung down her back to between her shoulder blades. Beatrice wore her hair pinned into a bun at her nape, her dress was a light tan with a tartan vest and sturdy boots on her feet.

"Must I go fetch him?" Ella started to stand when Gideon strolled into the dining room.

He looked to them and yawned widely. "I could have slept much longer," he announced.

"I am glad to see that at least ye are dressed. Do not forget ye promised to take us to the village this morning," Ella reminded him while looking him over.

Gideon yawned again. "I wish for nothing more than to return to my bed."

"If only we could all take such luxuries," Caelan said as he walked in. Unlike his brother, he looked to have been up for a while. Every strand of his reddish hair perfectly in place and dressed in what she could only describe as English attire, he lowered into a chair, stretched out his legs, and crossed his booted ankles.

A maid entered, and he asked for a cup of tea. "I have already eaten," he explained to them.

Caelan took both her and Ella in. "Good morning Miss Beatrice. Sister. What are yer plans for the day?"

"Good morning," Beatrice replied and looked to Ella.

"We are going to the village. There is a festival and Gideon is escorting us," Ella informed her brother. "Would ye like to come with us?"

"Ye know I cannot," Caelan replied with a droll look. "There is nothing about a festival that interests me."

"What does interest ye?" Beatrice asked and took a bite of bread.

Gideon huffed. "Long boring conversations with old men about the political state of the country and such."

"Ye should take heed and pay more attention to such things." The older brother gave Gideon a sharp look and then met Beatrice's gaze. "I prefer pursuits such as hunting,

20

competing, riding, and yes, I do enjoy conversations about topics that affect us."

"Such as?" Beatrice was intrigued.

"The monarchy's ever-changing mandates and philosophy," Caelan replied.

The man was not like any highlander she'd met. The only men who seemed to enjoy topics of philosophy and such were often older men, lowlanders, or Englishmen, which she preferred not to hold company with.

"Interesting," Beatrice replied.

"He is not a true highlander," Ella said shaking her head. "Spent too much time studying in the lowlands and doing whatever it is his mother insisted he do."

Caelan gave Ella a patient look and then met Beatrice's gaze. "Mother wished for me to be educated. She believes in the expansion of one's mind, Miss Beatrice."

"We of small minds must prepare to go," Gideon said standing. "Brother, I informed Ewan that I'd be gone to the village today. He will be here shortly to assist ye in whatever tasks necessary."

Caelan was serving as clan laird since his older brothers were gone. As a bastard son, most families would not consider it. However, Darach Ross had insisted that Caelan be treated the same as the rest of them were. Therefore, being third born, he took the duty of laird in Darach and Duncan's absence.

It seemed to Beatrice that Ewan and Gideon didn't mind one bit.

"If Ewan does not appear, I have the council," Caelan replied lifting a cup to his lips.

A proper gentleman Caelan stood when she and Ella did.

He remained silent as they hurried out.

"Hurry before Caelan decides we need tutoring," Ella exclaimed tugging her toward the great hall. It proved impossible to stifle a giggle.

MUCH LIKE MOST Scottish villages, the one nearest to the keep had a collection of two-story buildings that faced each other around a large square. From poles on the upstairs windows, colorful streamers waved gaily in the breeze.

Shop keepers had tied ribbons to their shingles adding to the colorful display.

People hurried up the center road, some pulling small wagons overfilled with items they hoped to sell or give out.

Lively music played and a few children held hands and danced in circles. Some older people joined in the melee as well.

Too excited to wait for Gideon, Beatrice and Ella hurried to the square wanting to see everything and to take part in all the games and activities.

As they made their way from one place to another, people greeted Ella, some asking about her brothers, others about her mother. Although studying her with curiosity, no one dared to ask who Beatrice was until Ella introduced her.

"We should shop first before finding a place to sit and enjoy the entertainment," a breathless Ella exclaimed. "Time will go by fast and we must make the most out of each minute."

They went from one stall to another. Ella purchased something from almost everyone, even if it was only something minute.

Several men gathered on the opposite side of the square. By their clothes, it was obvious they were not villagers, but perhaps landowners or from other clans.

Both she and Ella pretended interest in their purchases while studying the men from under their lashes.

"The one who just stretched is attractive," Ella whispered as they made their way back to the carriage to deposit their purchases.

Beatrice wrinkled her nose. "He did that on purpose to attract attention. The one next to him with light hair. He is far more fetching."

"Hmmm," Ella turned over her shoulder and then gasped softly. "He caught me looking. Aye, I agree. He is quite bonnie."

FINALLY, AFTER DROPPING off items into the carriage, they went to find a place to sit and watch the festivities. A group of dancers performed a lively and complicated dance, their feet moving so fast, it was fascinating.

"I find it interesting that ye are so well-liked. I thought the people of the village did not fully trust yer family," Beatrice said to Ella.

Her friend sighed. "Aye, it's true. They do not trust my family. However, Mother and I have always spent time here in the village doing what we can for the poor and the widowed. No matter how badly Father treated the people, or perhaps because of it, we did our best to help where we could."

"It must have been very difficult for ye," Beatrice said.

"It was. Still is in a way. I find that without this work, I am not sure what my place in the family is."

Beatrice believed that because she was the daughter of a powerful man and Ella the sister of one, they'd become close. Other than a future of marriage to whomever their family decided, neither she nor Ella had a true purpose.

Beatrice scanned the square, noting young women walking around the area, arms linked pretending not to notice the men who watched them with interest. Here and there a brave man would approach the women making small talk.

Most village women had a say in who they'd marry and form a family with. There was the occasional father who would orchestrate an agreement for benefit, but for the most part, it wasn't so.

Upon noting a couple sitting together talking, the young woman blushing at something the man said, Beatrice felt a pang of sadness that she'd never experience the simple act of getting to know someone just because.

"Here comes Gideon," Ella said looking around as if considering hiding from her brother. "I hope he does not insist we leave so soon."

Upon reaching them, Gideon sat and looked across the square. Beatrice studied his profile. He had dark brown hair, an aristocratic nose, and a strong chin. And like his brothers, he was tall and quite handsome. Many women watched him, but he seemed oblivious.

Beatrice suspected he was fully aware that by walking across the square and sitting with her and Ella, he'd attract attention.

And not just that of the women, but also as a warning to

any man who considered approaching them.

The hours flew by. They'd danced and laughed and strolled around the square. One man had actually spoken to Ella, which made them both giddy with excitement.

By the time they decided to head back to Keep Ross, the sun was setting and most of the revelers had headed to their homes. The only ones who remained were people who had enbibed too much ale.

"It was quite an enjoyable way to spend the day," Beatrice said to Ella as they settled into the carriage. "I do not believe I've ever spent so much time at a festival before."

Ella grinned. "We always spend the entire day. Gideon and I. Sometimes we drag Mother along."

"What of Duncan? Do ye and he do anything together?"

There was an instant change to Ella's expression. Something akin to sadness. "No, Duncan does not like crowds or large gatherings for that matter."

"What does he do with all his time?"

Her friend met Beatrice's gaze for a moment. "My brother is a kind and noble man… he is a loner, and it is something we have all come to accept."

It was obvious that Ella changed midsentence what she was going to say. If Duncan had secrets that only his family knew, then Beatrice accepted they needed no reason not to share them with her.

She was anxious to ask what the man in the village had said to Ella, but she dared not ask in front of Gideon. The topic would have to wait until they were alone.

Upon returning to the keep, Beatrice realized that the Ross men had not returned yet from North Uist. She was both disappointed and glad.

One more night of not knowing what her mother's response to her letter was a bit of an annoyance; however, it was best she get a good night's rest because the next day, Duncan and Stuart would surely return.

THE SCREAMS OF gulls woke Beatrice. She sat up in the bed and blinked at the bright sunlight entering through the window. She must have slept in quite late by the tray of food that was set on a table by the fireplace.

After a long day at the festival, she'd been exhausted. Slipping from the bed, she hurried to the window. Although it was a distance away, it would be possible to spot if the Ross men had returned.

There was activity at the seashore. Horses and men meandered. There was a line of birlinns that had not been there the day before.

Duncan and Stuart must have returned.

Leaning forward and squinting, Beatrice did her best to see who mounted on horses, but it was hard to tell. However, it was obvious her mother did not travel with them as there was no carriage and her mother would not ride astride.

Beatrice let out a long sigh and turned away. She dressed hurriedly, wishing to head downstairs in order to find out what news they brought back.

A maid, Orla, hurried in and looked first to her and then the tray. "Ye did not eat yet miss. The food will be cold."

"I just now woke. Thank ye for bringing it. I will eat a bit later. For now, I must dress."

Orla had been assigned to her since Annis, her former

maid now concentrated exclusively on Isobel. Her sister had taken Annis to Barra with her, so it left Beatrice to do for herself.

"Which dress would ye like?"

Beatrice eyed all the pastel gowns, they felt so out of place there at Keep Ross, where Ella and her mother, Lady Mariel, preferred earth tones.

"The green," she said and removed her nightdress.

Moments later, she waited impatiently for Orla to finish braiding her hair. When the maid was finally done, Beatrice smiled widely. "I love it."

The tray was cleared, and Beatrice took a deep breath before leaving her bedchamber. Hoping to find Ella, she hurried down the corridor.

To her chagrin, Ella was nowhere to be found. Not in her bedchamber, the great hall, or the family dining room. Finally, Beatrice walked into the kitchen. "Has anyone seen Miss Ella?"

The cook, Greer, and the helpers all shook their heads.

"I believe she may have gone to greet her brothers," a chambermaid said.

Beatrice hurried back through the great hall and out to the front door to keep watch. They would be arriving any moment and she had to know what would happen to her.

A thought struck. Perhaps they'd sent one of her brothers to fetch her. Beatrice lifted her skirts, ran through the great hall and back up to her bedchamber. She was not ready to return. Not yet.

As the party got closer, Beatrice took in each person. Stuart rode ahead, Ella beside him. There were several guardsmen who rode behind them, everyone riding at a slow leisurely pace.

Neither Duncan nor her brothers were with the arriving party. Beatrice let out a slow breath. Perhaps all was well. No one came for her and therefore her mother must have decided to let her remain for a while longer.

This would give her time to write another letter to let her know there was no courtship, and all would end well.

With a wide smile, she made her way down the stairs to greet Stuart and get information about her family.

Stuart entered, his hazel gaze meeting hers with a curious look. "My brother wishes to speak to ye. He had to go to his home, but will return in a day or two."

"Oh," Beatrice pretended to be surprised. "Why would yer brother wish to speak to me?"

Stuart shrugged. "From yer mother." He handed her a wrinkled letter that he pulled from a sack he carried.

"Ye must see what yer mother wrote," Ella said tugging her to the parlor. "I wonder if she is cross?"

"In all probability she is furious. I feel a bit guilty for not returning home," Beatrice replied and meant it.

Before tearing the letter open, she let out a deep breath. "I hate to disappoint my parents."

"Read it," Ella prodded.

The letter was short. The words were troubling.

"She will come to fetch me shortly. She waits until after a visit from the MacLeod."

Ella waited quietly, so Beatrice continued. "She is angry and points out that my overextended visit is very rude."

"I am sure all will be well once she sees that we wished for ye to remain," Ella said with a bright smile. "Do not worry yerself."

When Ella left to see about a meal for her brothers, Beatrice continued reading the letter.

> *Yer father and I think it best that ye marry a MacLeod. Ye must put off any plans between ye and Duncan Ross.*
>
> *For now, we will not discuss a marriage agreement while the MacLeod's visit. However, once ye return it will be the first thing to be dealt with.*
>
> *End things immediately and do not give Duncan Ross any reason to think ye and he will marry.*

Beatrice stared at the words and pondered at marriage to a MacLeod. Which one did her parents plan to marry her to? She couldn't picture what the MacLeod's sons looked like. When younger, they'd been unremarkable.

The alliance between her clan and the MacLeod's had become stronger since they'd united to fight against northern aggression. As expected, since Isobel had married a Ross, it was she that would be offered up to a MacLeod.

Like a form of payment, she would be offered as a token.

She'd speak to Duncan as soon as possible. Perhaps convince Ella to take her to his home the following day. It was best to clear things up and ensure there were no misunderstandings. Already she'd acted like a spoiled child by remaining at Keep Ross much longer than necessary. Now it was time to act like an adult and face the consequences of her actions.

Marriage in the coming months meant she'd be busy through the fall and winter as her parents would probably plan a spring wedding.

She let out a long sigh and stared out the window. When Duncan had come to inform her that he was to escort her home, why hadn't she just accepted?

Now it felt as if she could not stand to think about returning. As much as she missed her parents and her home, the idea that she'd only be there for a few months prior to marrying was too finite.

A tear trickled down her cheek, sliding all the way to the edge of her face.

If only there was a way to be free. To live her life in North Uist at home, helping her mother, and spending the days doing as she wished.

Of course, once Evander married, it would be his wife who would work closely with her mother and be the one in charge of the staff duties. There would be no place for her.

Depending on who Beatrice married would determine what her place in a home would be. The thought of not knowing anything about her future was daunting.

Moments later, Beatrice found Ella sitting in the great room at a table surrounded by several servants.

"Ye should ensure the beds are made and bedchambers swept," Ella instructed an older woman, who hurried off. "And ye, let the laundresses know that new linens should be placed on the laird's bed as well as Mother's."

As the servants got their orders, they went off to do as told. Beatrice looked to the open book in front of Ella. It was a ledger of sorts.

"Hello friend," Ella said greeting her. "I am afraid, to be very much behind in my duties because of yesterday."

Beatrice sat across the table from her. "I understand.

Sometimes I help Mother run the household because missing just one day will ruin an entire week."

While Ella worked, Beatrice ate a light meal, in her mind formulating ways to escape the mundane life that awaited her in North Uist, or further north on the Isle of Lewis if her parents had their way.

It was time to take matters in hand. First, she had to speak to Duncan and find out exactly what was said between him and her mother.

"Ella? Where does Duncan live?"

CHAPTER THREE

THE EMPTINESS OF the large house was perfect. Duncan sat at a large table alone and ate a simple meal of meat and potatoes that Gara, the cook and housekeeper, served for him.

Other than a pair of servants, he and Caelan lived in the house alone.

There were few decorations on the walls or surfaces. What there was had been brought and placed by his mother and sister, who seemed to think a tapestry on the wall or embroidered pillow were a necessary item in every household.

Once a season, his mother and Ella would appear with a troupe of servants. They would scour the house top to bottom, airing out bedding and pillows and displacing every spider from their roosts in the corners.

His housekeeper would beam for days after, since she oversaw the servants who cleaned out the kitchens, dining room, and larders.

If Duncan had his way, he'd prefer to live away from even the few servants they had, not having to hide on the days when his attacks were so severe, he could not hear or see anything other than the horrors of his past.

"It is a beautiful day outside," Gara announced. "I will be in the garden with Firtha if ye wish to find us."

"Very well," Duncan replied. "Do not worry about another

meal. I will eat the same thing later if I become hungry. Caelan will remain at the keep for another few days."

Gara was an older woman who'd worked at Keep Ross for many years before being offered the position there at his house. She was widowed and with only one daughter, Firtha, whom she'd brought along with her.

Quiet by nature, Gara was a perfect fit at his house. She and Firtha would spend hours gardening, sewing, or sometimes visiting in the kitchen with friends who would stop by on occasion. Often the woman proclaimed to having a rich life there and Duncan was glad for her.

Admittedly, both she and Firtha were given large well-furnished bedchambers. In Duncan's estimation, they earned it, having to do all the work required.

There was a man name Creagh, who looked after their horses and the few livestock, but other than that, Duncan preferred to not hire more help.

He continued eating, enjoying the silence while considering if he would spend the afternoon working on a wall he was constructing or wait until the next day.

There was a light knocking sound and he turned toward the front of the house. He waited, but the silence stretched. He considered if perhaps an animal was testing the door to see if it could enter.

When the sound happened again, Duncan stood and walked to the front of the room. Peering out the window, he caught sight of a horse that had been tethered. The animal's tail swished side to side, as it nibbled on grass.

It was Ella's horse. Why would his sister ride out alone to see him?

Hurrying to the front door, he yanked it opened prepared to scold his sister. However, the pair of wide blue eyes peering up at him did not belong to his sister.

Beatrice Macdonald gave him a worried look and took a step back. "I need to speak to ye. It is very important."

For a long moment, he wasn't sure what to do. Invite her in or send her on her way. Of course, if he sent her away, he'd have to accompany her.

"Who escorted ye here?"

She shook her head. "No one, I came alone. It is a direct route. It was quite easy to find this home."

"It is not safe for ye to be out unescorted. Why did ye not bring a guard with ye?"

Leaning to the side, she peered around him. "May I come inside?"

Duncan stepped back and motioned for her to enter. Then once again he scanned the outdoors, unable to believe the woman had traveled the distance to his home unescorted through unfamiliar land.

When he turned, she had removed her light cloak and blew out a breath. "It is unseasonably warm is it not? Then again, I am not familiar with South Uist... is it always this warm in the summer?"

When she eyed his cup of ale, he motioned for her to drink. "Ye can have it."

"Oh, thank ye, I am quite parched."

While she drank, Duncan looked her over to ensure she was not injured. Other than a tear at the bottom of her skirts, she seemed well enough. Her hair was a bit disheveled, the blond waves framing her face in a wild uncontrolled manner.

She was flushed from the ride, her cheeks bright pink and her eyes sparkled with curiosity as she took in the surroundings.

"Yer sister told me ye would be here because ye rarely go anywhere. So, I took a chance to come and speak to ye. Now that I consider it, I should have asked for an escort. However, everyone is so busy at the keep. I hate to be a bother…" She stopped talking and met his gaze.

"I am interrupting yer meal. Please sit. Eat. I already ate before leaving."

In truth he was hungry, so after motioning for Beatrice to sit, he poured more ale for her and lowered to his chair.

"What brings ye here?" he asked and began to eat again.

Beatrice let out a long sigh. "First of all, I wish to apologize to ye for writing to Mother and stating ye were courting me."

"Why did ye?"

Seeming to realize that perhaps her hair was out of place, she brushed her hands over the strands, attempting to smooth them. "I had to come up with an excuse to remain longer. It was the only thing that occurred to me."

"Why me?"

The question seemed to surprise Beatrice, her brows lowering as she considered how to reply. "Ye are never at the keep and I figured Mother would find ye too intimidating to question."

Duncan gave her a dubious look. "Ye do not seem to have any hesitance to approach me."

Lifting the cup and holding it with both hands, it was as if she tried to hide her expression from him. "I do. In a way find ye a bit… unapproachable."

"I see."

When he continued eating in silence, Duncan could feel her studying him. He had to admit it was a bit enjoyable to keep the mischievous lass wondering what he'd say next. "Yer mother asked my intentions."

Duncan met her wide gaze, purposely not saying anything else. Her plump lips parted while she waited for him to continue.

"I told her ye were someone I'd be proud to court."

"What?" Beatrice leaned forward. "She believed it then?"

"I could not very well tell yer mother, ye were lying."

Her bottom lip disappeared when she bit it. "Oh, dear. Thank ye. Again, I apologize."

Duncan nodded. "Now we must discuss how ye will return to Dún Láidir. Ye cannot go alone, and I do not have time to take ye."

"I do not require an escort. I am an able rider. I will ride there directly. Do not bother yerself."

The only plans he had was to work on the wall at the back of the property. Lifting and stacking the heavy stones not only kept him fit and strong, but also seemed to keep his mind away from dark things.

Not in the mood to travel to Keep Ross, he wondered if he should ask the stableman to escort Beatrice back.

"Would ye mind showing me about?" Beatrice asked. "This is a most beautiful home."

If the minx was up to something, he did not detect it. She seemed genuinely interested in the house.

"Of course," he said pushing his empty plate away.

They walked side-by-side from the main hall to the opposite side, where he showed her Caelan's study and across the hall, a small parlor. Just down the corridor was two small bedchambers that were rarely used.

Next, he guided her up a stairwell where his and Caelan's bedchambers were as well as a large room that their mother used when visiting. There was another guest room and a small chamber that could be used as a sitting room. Currently, there were only a pair of chairs in there.

Beatrice went to a window and peered out. "I find it interesting that ye do not live with a view of the sea. I do adore the views from the keep."

It was best for him to not have such a view. The memories of time at sea were not ones he cherished. Unfortunately, many times his family business forced him to travel to other Isles, which meant going by bìrlinn. If he had his way, he would remain landside.

"I prefer the view of forests and land."

Beatrice turned from the window and looked at a painting on the wall. It was a small depiction of a field. "Who did this? It is beautiful."

"My mother."

A wide smile spread over her pretty face almost making him smile in return. "I was not aware she was so talented."

He looked at the painting, seeing it through her eyes. Flowers grew wildly in a field that had a cusp of trees in the distance. In the sky a pair of birds flew across the expanse, giving the illusion of unending space.

"Would ye like to see the outdoors?"

"I would," Beatrice replied, tearing her eyes away from the painting.

He led her down the stairs and out the side door by the kitchens.

Gara and Firtha straightened, from their gardening, with shocked looks when seeing him with Beatrice. The housekeeper jumped to her feet and rushed to them. "I apologize Mister Duncan. I wasn't aware there was a visitor. I will brew some tea..."

"Do not worry yerself," Beatrice said with a soft smile. "I have already partaken of Mister Duncan's ale."

The housekeeper looked to Duncan. "Would ye like me to prepare a meal?"

"No, we are going for a short walk and then Miss Beatrice is leaving," he replied.

The women remained still as statues, watching them as they walked away.

"Ye only have two servants?" Beatrice asked.

"There are two more. Creagh, a man who looks after the horses, and sometimes a lad comes and helps him."

She looked up at him with curiosity. "I suppose ye and Caelan do not require much then?"

"My brother would have a much larger staff, if given the choice. However, he agrees with me that we do not have a need for so many people about."

Duncan had to admit to feeling at ease as he walked Beatrice around the sides and back of the house to show her the land. Something about her was different than other women. She didn't seem to want anything from him other than company. Her curiosity was genuine as she gazed across the area, leaning forward, and rising to her toes, she pointed to the wall he'd been working on for over a year.

"Why is there a partial wall there?" She looked up to him, her clear gaze seeming to see much deeper than he would prefer.

Uneven, some portions higher than others, the wall was not exactly a work of art. If anything, it was an eyesore, with its haphazard shape and piles of stones around it.

"I work on it for exercise. To keep in shape for the games. As ye may have seen, I compete in the caber toss and stone throw."

Intelligent eyes scanned his face for a moment and then she turned to the wall. "I see. Ye should at least make it look somewhat straight. It is visible from the house is it not?"

He almost laughed. Only a woman would care how a stone wall looked. Especially one that did not serve any true purpose.

"I may actually move it to over there," he pointed to an area to the left. "Use the stones to wall in the space so it can be an enclosed garden."

Beatrice shrugged. "I suppose if ye use it for training, then it matters not where ye build it." Moving away, she turned back to the house. "It is a pity ye do not have a larger staff and entertain. The house is beautiful. The land flat and perfect for a gathering."

A shudder ran through him at the thought of having groups of people about. Even before he'd become reclusive, he'd never been one for crowds. As a lad, he'd been shy and not as boisterous as his brothers.

"Ye are not one for company are ye?" Beatrice asked. "Some people prefer solitude. Although I have a hard time understanding it, I accept that not everyone wants the company of others."

She then looked up to the sky. "Goodness, I best be heading back. Clouds are gathering and I do not wish to be caught in a storm."

"I will escort ye back," Duncan said not quite happy about going back to the keep. He'd be forced to remain the night by the way the clouds were gathering.

"Ye will not. I have already put ye out. I assure ye to be fine. I will ride fast and be back at the keep before very long." Beatrice lifted her skirts and hurried back toward the house, every so often looking up at the sky.

He followed walking slower and wondering why she found it necessary to come in the first place. He'd told Stuart to inform her he'd come there so they could speak prior to her mother coming and demanding he marry her.

Had they even come up with a plan? He couldn't remember much as he studied the woman in front of him. She was beautiful. In all probability the loveliest creature he'd ever seen.

It only took a few moments to saddle his horse and by the time Beatrice emerged from the house with her cloak on, he waited for her.

Her eyes widened. "I keep telling myself to stop being so impulsive, but then I do something without thinking it through. Now I am infringing on yer time."

"We have not discussed what we will do when yer mother comes," Duncan said as he took her by the waist and lifted the woman to her horse. It was hard to ignore the feel of her body under his hands and the soft fragrance from her clothing as she arranged herself atop the horse.

Once he mounted, they began riding toward his family

home. With each moment that passed, the clouds became darker and soon he realized they would not be able to outride the storm.

There were two options: attempt to ride through a downpour; or find shelter.

Duncan looked to Beatrice, who gave him a worried look. "There is a place just over the bend where we can find shelter from the rain. Hopefully, it will not last too long."

They rode to an abandoned place that had often been used by men to gather or hide. He prayed there was nothing too unfavorable in the place when they entered.

The skies rumbled and as soon as they reached the empty building, a downpour began.

CHAPTER FOUR

D ESPITE NOT HAVING to ride far in the rain, by the time they came to the dilapidated house, Beatrice was soaked through and shivering.

After pulling the horses to a covered area, Beatrice watched as Duncan pushed a door open. Thankfully with him along, she felt safe to enter what looked to be a rather intimidating place.

The air was musty, but thankfully the room was dry. There was a fireplace, and Duncan hurried out to find some kindling to build a fire to warm up and dry their clothes with.

It was only a few moments later that a cheery fire burned in the hearth and both Beatrice and Duncan hovered close to it, holding their hands out. He'd taken a branch and cut off the smaller twigs and leaves then fashioned it between a broken chair and a table so that Beatrice could hang her cloak on it to dry. Unfortunately, her dress was wet as well, so she stood by the fire hoping the heat would dry most of the wetness away.

"I am not sure how long the rain will continue," Duncan said unfolding a plaid he'd brought and kept in a bag on his saddle. "Ye can undress and wrap in this so that we can attempt to dry yer clothes. I will go see about the horses."

He handed her the plaid and walked out into the rain before Beatrice could stop him. He could have just gone to the opposite side of the room and turned his back, now the man would return soaked.

It was best to hurry, so she removed her wet dress and shift and wrapped the plaid around her waist, and expertly pulled the front and back up to tie at the shoulders making a dress that covered her well. The fabric fell from the knots to cover her arms and the bottom of it fell to her ankles.

Makeshift dress completed, she rushed to the door. "Duncan, please come inside." Her voice got lost with the storm. But just a moment later, he appeared from the back of the house drenched.

"I pulled the horses into a back room. They will be dry there." He took in her appearance with a look of approval that made her insides giddy. "This is not the first time ye have had to wear a plaid to cover up."

Beatrice huffed at the implication. "My mother taught us how after trips to the seaside. Often our clothing ended up wet or dirty. It is a necessary trick for women of the isles."

With a nod, he brushed past to near the fire. Beatrice did her best to ignore how the wet tunic clung to his muscular back and arms.

After draping her gown and other clothes to dry, Beatrice settled on the floor on a makeshift pallet that had already been in the room that Duncan draped his bag from the saddle atop. He sat on a stool and stared into the fire in silence.

Beatrice wasn't sure what she could say about the situation. It was all her fault of course and now if someone found out they were alone, in a building with her undressed, the consequences could be high. She studied the quiet man for a moment, unsure how to begin the uncomfortable conversation.

Seeming to sense her regard he looked to her. "Ye want to say something, but struggle? Somehow I find it hard to believe."

He joked. At a time like this. It could be he had not realized the predicament she'd put them in. Yes, that had to be it. If she brought it up, then how would he react?

"It is just that… well, I have put ye into yet another situation." Beatrice let out a breath. "Please forgive me."

He frowned. "The storm will pass, and we will be on our way. It is still early in the day. I am sure it will stop raining before dark."

Did he think her scared of the storm? "Ye are aware that if it does not, and it is found out we spent time here alone, the consequences could be dire?"

"No one will ever dictate to me what I must do," he replied with nonchalance. "Ye should stop worrying yerself and rest."

Beatrice huffed. "I do not need to rest. I am perfectly rested, I assure ye. I will have to insist that ye take our situation with more seriousness."

A SOFT SOUND stirred Beatrice and she woke with a start. She'd fallen asleep curled up on the pallet. With a gasp, she sat up. Outside the rain continued and it was quite worrisome. However, what was worse was that it was dark outside.

Night had come and they were still in the abandoned house.

Alone. Together.

"Duncan?" She blinked at the fire first and then around the room. He was not there. Beatrice gasped again. Had he waited for her to fall asleep and then left? She jumped to her feet and ran to the door. When she opened it, the cold rain made her step backward and she closed the door.

Where had the man gone? Surely he'd not left her alone to be found by bad men, who could bring her harm.

She crossed her arms as anger surged. "He will pay for this." Hurrying to where her dress hung, she felt it and was relieved to find it fully dry. Her shift was dry as well. Beatrice untied the plaid and let it fall to the floor, then standing before the fire fully bare, she grabbed the shift from the branch, turned toward the fire, and gasped.

Duncan sat on the stool, back to the wall, his gaze moving over her body.

"Ahhh!" Beatrice held the flimsy shift in front of herself and screamed. "Why did ye not make noise to tell me ye were there?"

"I thought ye saw me," he replied and once again gave her the once-over. "Why are ye angry?"

Beatrice sputtered, "I-I, ye… ye're here and I am un-dressed."

A frown was followed by a shrug. It occurred to Beatrice that he did not seem at all surprised nor discomfited by her nudity. If anything, she would have expected him to attempt something, to make advances. Instead, he remained sitting and looked at her as if were an everyday occurrence.

"Turn yer head," she finally spat. "I cannot believe this."

He turned and she quickly pulled her shift over her head allowing the folds to fall past her hips and down to her knees. When she looked over to him, Duncan had his head turned away, but his eyes where still on her.

"Ye are looking." She stomped to where he was and hit him on the shoulder as hard as she could. "How dare ye."

To her further annoyance, he grunted and gave her a bland look. "How could I not?"

Beatrice was at a loss for words. In truth, if the roles were reversed, she would definitely be watching him. She'd never seen a man fully bereft of clothing. However, she suspected the man in the room had seen more than his fair share.

Instead of arguing further, she went back to where her clothes were and continued to get dressed. "We should head back to the keep. Everyone must be worried sick."

He pointed to the ceiling. "It's still storming. I am hopeful it will lessen enough at sunrise that we can continue there."

"Do ye realize the implications if it is found out that we spent the night together all alone?" Beatrice fumbled with the ties of her bodice and gave up. At this point what did propriety matter, the man had seen her fully naked. "My family would demand ye marry me immediately."

"We will not tell them then," Duncan said, and for some reason it stung that he did not wish to marry her. There was nothing about a marriage between them that would be so horrible. The families were already tied, she would be able to spend time with her sister and best of all, not have to marry a MacLeod and live in the frozen north.

She let out an annoyed sigh and lowered back to the pallet. "And how do ye plan to explain us appearing at the keep together?"

"Ye left my house, without telling me. I was on my way to the keep and happened upon ye."

His explanation had merit. After all, she was resourceful

enough to have found an abandoned place to spend the night. In reality, she would have continued riding through the rain, ended up lost, and probably have caught her death from the cold. It was best not to think on that alternate outcome.

"Fine. I agree to that explanation." Outside the rain continued to fall. By the sound of it, the storm was lessening. Beatrice decided to rest until they left, so she pulled the plaid over her and snuggled into it.

She looked to Duncan. "Who do ye plan to marry one day?"

There was a hardening to his expression. "I do not plan to marry—ever."

"Ye must wish to have bairns and a wife to care for ye."

"Nay."

Beatrice sat up. She'd never met someone who planned to end up alone. "What about when ye grow old? Ye will be alone."

He gave her a droll look. "I have six siblings. They will marry and have children. Surely one of their offspring will look after an old uncle." His response was flat as if he didn't believe it. How sad that someone would give up on life and all that it might bring and expect to end their time here alone.

"Ye are still young. There is time to change yer mind," Beatrice told him, more to make herself feel better than for his benefit.

"Why are ye avoiding returning to North Uist?"

Lifting to sit, Beatrice considered her answer. "I do not wish to be used as an object, to be traded to a man in exchange for some sort of agreement between clans. My father plans to marry me off to a MacLeod. I prefer to choose my own husband."

"Ye have known all yer life it was not a possibility," Duncan told her what she already knew. "Why rebel?"

"Because I have to. Ye of all people should see that. I wish to marry a man I admire and am attracted to. Someone who I can share how I feel and who listens to me. Truly listens. I imagine the MacLeod's to be much the same as most men."

Duncan shrugged. "I am sure they too have been groomed to marry someone that is chosen for them and perhaps have accepted it."

For some reason, sadness enveloped her and Beatrice closed her eyes as tears threatened. "I wish that things were different, but I cannot change my future. I cannot be a disappointment to my parents. Yer right. I should just accept my lot." She wiped at a tear and drew in a ragged breath.

"Are ye crying?" Duncan leaned forward and studied her face.

"No," Beatrice lied. "Smoke from the fire got in my eyes." Once again, she settled onto the pallet and in her mind pictured that the abandoned house was where she and Duncan lived. She imagined where she'd place furniture and that they often had long conversations before retiring for the evening.

He would envelop her in his strong arms at night and keep her safe from the outside world. Nothing or no one would dare interrupt their life.

"Ye will be well," Duncan said lowering next to her and pulling her against his chest.

It was then Beatrice realized she'd been sobbing. His actions only made her cry harder in the knowledge that once her mother arrived, she would return home and be quickly married off. Her freedom and life would be forever changed.

Duncan was silent. He didn't try to soothe or calm her, but his quiet strength gave Beatrice comfort, and she finally stopped the tears.

"Thank ye," she whispered and let out a shaky sigh. "I know what I must do and will return home once my mother arrives." Instead of moving away, she snuggled against his warm body and promptly fell asleep.

DUNCAN HAD NEVER held a woman while she slept. The few times he'd been intimate had been a fast interlude. A quick pulling up of skirts and lowering of breeches, no romance, only physical release.

The picture of Beatrice's body was singed in his mind. He'd never seen a woman fully bereft of clothing and now he was sure he had seen perfection. Her breathtaking beauty stealing his breath and leaving him unable to warn her of his presence.

Her creamy skin didn't contain a single blemish or mark, and her breasts were pert, with dark pink tips. She had a slender waist that flared out slightly to hips, which led down to legs that were delicate like her. He'd caught sight of the patch of dark blond hair at the apex of her sex, a place that claimed his attention and caused an immediate reaction.

WHEN SHE STIRRED, he inhaled her hair feeling out of place while holding the slight woman against his large, scarred body. Someone like her should not find comfort in the likes of him. He was unclean, not just physically, but internally as well.

Beatrice was to marry a MacLeod. He tried to picture the

brothers. It had been years since he'd seen either of them at a competition. From what he recalled, the youngest was a rather large man. He'd competed against Duncan in the caber toss. But other than a few words, he'd not spent much time with him.

The eldest he recalled a bit better. He'd become drunk and gotten into a brawl during the festivities. It had taken several men to pull him off the man he was beating. He hoped Beatrice would not be marrying him and be subjected to his horrible temper.

It was hard to imagine the beauty in his arms married to either man. Neither deserved someone like her. Beatrice deserved a man who would allow her freedom to explore. With an impulsive nature, she would always be getting into situations, so the beauty did have to be kept protected, but not so much to hinder her adventurous spirit.

If he could, he would marry her just to set her free to be and do as she wished.

If only he could.

However, the beast within would never allow it. A relationship of any kind could only bring disastrous results. And he could never subject anyone, especially not someone as special as Beatrice Macdonald to it.

CHAPTER FIVE

THE STORM HAD made it almost impossible to ride through the night. Thankfully the rain slowed to a drizzle and Farlan Reid got out from the makeshift shelter he'd made and stretched. The fact he'd spent a horrible night only made him more determined to find Duncan Ross and make him pay dearly for it.

It may have taken him years to find his way to South Uist, but now that he was so close to finally getting revenge, he had to do his best to keep his wits.

First, he'd find a tavern, eat, get dry clothes, and purchase a horse. Then, he'd track down Duncan. The man would not expect to see him, as he probably believed him dead.

Farlan's lips curved. "They did not kill me, Duncan Ross. Ye will wish they did."

After walking for several hours, he made it to a small village and walked into the tavern. Probably due to the storm and because it was still early, there was no one other than one man there.

"What can I do fer ye?" the man inquired as soon as Farlan walked in.

"Ale, and some food." Farlan took the man in. "I would pay ye for some clothes as well."

The man nodded. "Aye, there's some extra things upstairs

in the room on the right. Help yerself to what fits."

Moments later, feeling better in dry clothes, Farlan returned downstairs and ate the simple fare the man provided as well as a cup of ale.

When he started to pay, the tavern owner held up a hand. "No payment sir. I do what I can to help those in need. Now ye go and help someone who needs it."

Farlan wanted to laugh. The only reason he'd traveled so far was to find and make a man pay for betraying him. "Where can I purchase a horse?"

After placing coins on a table surface, Farlan walked out to find the farmer, the tavern owner had spoken of. If the day continued to be as easy, perhaps he would find Duncan soon.

He'd not asked the tavern owner where to find his old friend, because the last thing he needed was to alert the Ross clan that someone looked for them. No, he'd have to go forward with care. He was on Ross territory and it would be too easy to be caught.

THANKFULLY, THE RAIN had stopped, giving him a clearer view of the road ahead. It was only his second time on the Isle of North Uist, and he had to admit not caring for the surroundings. As much time as he'd spent at sea, when on land he preferred not to be surrounded by it. However, the familiarity of the salty air made him feel at home as he began his trek.

One thing he remembered about Duncan Ross, was that he preferred to be alone. Especially given the years they'd been acquainted. The many days they'd spent alone, tied up in the belly of a ship, fed scraps, and whipped until half dead.

Farlan shook his head in an effort to dislodge the memories. Then he took a breath and scanned the surroundings. No, it was best to keep the picture of the time with Duncan. How he'd grown to depend on the man, who'd taken beatings for him and shared what was left of their meager food in an effort to keep him alive. They'd shared so much. And then he'd betrayed him. The day had finally come that freedom was within reach and Duncan had abandoned him. Escaped alone and never returned for him.

That he lived was a miracle. After being starved for days, the ship's crew had taken great delight in tossing him overboard.

He'd finally found freedom, although he'd expected it was in death.

By some miracle he'd survived. Someone aboard the ship had taken mercy on him and tossed a plank of wood overboard. He'd clung to the wood for an entire night and been rescued by a group of fishermen.

Now, as he stared at the surroundings, Farlan contemplated his drive to seek revenge. He had nothing to live for. His family was gone. Upon returning to his home, he'd found an empty cottage; the villagers told him his young wife and bairn had been taken years earlier. He'd found them in a grave not far from the village. They'd been either killed or died of exposure.

Then upon seeking his sister, he found out she and their parents had succumbed to a horrible illness. Too afraid to catch what they'd had; the others had allowed them to die.

If he'd been free, if only Duncan had come for him, he would have been able to help. He would have been there to protect his family, his wife, and child.

Yes, it wasn't directly Duncan's fault, he was not so bitter that he didn't realize the crew that kidnapped him were the ones directly responsible. Ultimately, Farlan had dispensed his own justice. Killing them one by one. Waiting at the docks, taking his time to hunt them down, and ensuring they suffered before dying.

Those he didn't personally kill, were dead by other means. Now he only had one left. One person he held directly responsible for keeping him from saving his own.

A bird cawed overhead, pulling Farlan from his musings, as he spotted a young lad tugging a goat toward the village he'd come from.

The boy ignored him until Farlan called to him. "Aye, lad. I have a coin for ye, if ye help me find a friend."

"Sir?" The lad stopped and stared up at him.

"Do ye know where Duncan Ross lives?

The lad nodded eagerly; his gaze locked on the coin Farlan held up. "In the big house next to a loch." He pointed in the direction he'd come from.

Farlan tossed the lad a coin. "Go on now." The boy grinned up at him. "I can tell ye where the rest of the family live."

At the words, Farlan's breath hitched. It could be he was thinking of his revenge in the wrong manner. Taking what mattered from Duncan Ross first could be something far better than just killing the man.

"Where?"

The lad hesitated and Farlan dug out a pair of coins and tossed them at the lad. After picking them up the boy scratched his head.

"Past the big house in the next village." He pointed. "That way."

"No one must know we were alone together, we must ensure it," Beatrice repeated as they neared the keep. "My sister will be mortified if she were to find out that I was gone overnight."

Despite knowing nothing happened between them, Beatrice worried about how her sister would respond to knowing she'd done something so reckless. Goodness, sometimes she was appalled at her own behavior.

Duncan was quiet as he guided the horse. It was strange how despite the long stretches where he didn't speak, she found herself understanding what he thought by the way he held his head or how he looked at her.

"I think my sister will be most cross. Hopefully, by the time she returns, there will be enough of a time span that no one will inform her about this."

He gave her a look and she blew out a breath. "Yes, I know, it is wishful thinking on my part."

The gates opened and upon entering, Ella and Caelan hurried from the front of the house to them.

"What happened?" Ella looked her over, no doubt noticing her crumpled dress and mussed hair. "Where did ye go?"

Stealing a glance at Duncan, Beatrice swallowed. "I went to speak to Duncan and upon my return, alone, I ended up having to find refuge for the night when the storm hit."

Both Ella's and Caelan's eyes narrowed. It was obvious they didn't believe one word she'd uttered. Except perhaps that she'd gone to speak to Duncan.

It was more obvious when Ella spoke again, each word pronounced slowly. "Ye allowed her to return unaccompanied?"

"Then why did ye arrive together?"

Duncan gave Beatrice a droll look, giving her the opportunity to continue with her story that would surely hit upon unbelieving ears.

She slumped and let out a breath remaining silent.

The brothers seemed to have a silent communication. Caelan took his brother's appearance in, then slid a look to her.

Finally, he motioned to the front door. "We must speak."

The great room was empty. It was too early for villagers to come and seek an audience. Then again, since Darach was gone, there wouldn't be as many people coming.

"Where are Stuart and Gideon?" Beatrice asked.

Ella shrugged. "Gideon has not gotten out of bed. I suspect, he was up late partaking in too much whisky. Stuart is gone to Ewan's house to help with whatever is needed. Since Catriona is not well enough to get out of bed yet, Ewan must remain close to home."

It was a relief that the only ones at home were Ella and Caelan. Beatrice took her friend's hand. "My sister cannot know that I was gone all night. She will be most cross."

"Ye cannot expect to keep it from her," Ella said. "Too many people are aware of it. We searched the house and alerted the staff to look for ye. We learned ye had gone in the direction of the village when we questioned the guards."

"No one came looking for me."

"A villager told us ye arrived at Caelan and Duncan's home. When the storm began, Caelan supposed ye were sheltered at his house."

Beatrice sighed. "It is hard to remain secretive around these parts."

"It is," Ella replied with a chuckle. "People are very curious. Especially when it comes to someone they are not familiar with."

They went through the great hall and up the stairs to Beatrice's bedchamber. Once there, she quickly washed up and changed clothes into one of her more colorful gowns. She made a mental note to have a seamstress make her a pair of dresses in more muted tones. The light colors made her feel frivolous.

"What truly happened?" Ella asked as Beatrice brushed the tangles from her hair. "I know my brother can be somewhat... difficult."

"It was so thoughtless of me to seek him. I had to know what exactly happened when he delivered Mother's letter. What she'd said to him. I planned to find out and return immediately. Then that horrible storm hit."

Ella waited for her to continue.

Beatrice relented. She had to tell someone. "We were traveling back when the storm began, and we found shelter in an abandoned building. Yer brother made a fire for us and we slept until morning."

"Did anyone see ye go there? Alone? Together?"

"I am sure that if they did, the news will reach the keep soon enough. After all, ye did say the people about here are curious."

Ella wringed her hands. "Hopefully the rain kept the curious away."

"What do ye think will happen when Darach finds out?" Beatrice asked. "I am most fearful of his reaction."

By Ella's surprised expression, her friend had not considered it. "I honestly do not know. He has been laird for such a short time. He is being careful about every decision. We should go speak to Caelan and Duncan. I am sure they are having the very same conversation we are."

They went back down to the main floor of the keep. People had begun to trickle in, mostly it seemed to get a meal and sit about in the warmth of the indoor space. Many people, especially those who traveled, did not make accommodations and hoped to garner the favor of a place to rest there at the keep.

As they made their way to the family dining room to look for Caelan and Duncan, a boy hurried to Ella. He handed her a message and waited, his gaze darting to the tables.

"Go get something to eat. I will find ye later to give ye a coin." Ella smiled as the boy scampered off.

"Who sends ye notes via a child?" Beatrice asked, intrigued.

Ella shook her head. "Usually, it's my aunt who lives not too far. She often sends a boy to invite me for a visit."

"They have not visited since I've been here. Why?"

"Because she is my father's sister and like him is not kind to anyone. For whatever reason, she seems to enjoy my company. She and her spinster daughter are always eager for news of what happens with the family and the clan."

Upon entering the dining room, Caelan and Duncan

looked up. When Duncan's gaze clashed with hers, Beatrice felt a flutter in her stomach, her hand moving over the area.

"We must discuss what we will say to Darach and Isobel about this incident," Ella began immediately. "Someone may have seen them riding here and seeking shelter."

"It was storming," Duncan said. "I did not see anyone."

"That does not mean no one saw ye and Beatrice leaving this morning," Ella insisted.

Caelan motioned for them to sit. "Ye should eat. The food grows cold."

Once seated, Beatrice took a piece of bread and waited for Ella to pour the tea. She then slathered butter on her bread, lifted a thinly sliced piece of meat, and placed it atop the butter. When taking a healthy bite, she noted that Duncan watched her with a frown.

"Ye should try it. Very tasty," Beatrice said and took a second bite.

Ella emulated her and took a bite of her slice of bread. "It is indeed," she said between dainty bites.

"We will tell them the truth," Duncan said, with a challenging gaze at Beatrice. "There is nothing to hide from. We sought shelter and nothing untoward happened."

"It is not that simple and ye both know it," Caelan informed them. "Just the chance someone will report what happened and word gets to the Macdonald, could make things very complicated."

Beatrice was growing tired of the ramifications of her actions. She didn't mind having to deal with the consequences, but she didn't want Duncan to have to be embroiled in her mess. "I will ensure my parents are informed and that they understand nothing happened. It was a matter of necessity that we found ourselves alone."

When no one spoke, she continued. "My father is very understanding. He values honesty and will know that what I say is true."

While they ate, Ella told her brothers of the summons by her aunt before turning the discussion to the birth of Ewan and Catriona's second child. Though, truthfully, it was Caelan and Ella who did the speaking, with an occasional nod from Duncan.

While the Ross siblings discussed the situations of having to handle things until Darach returned, Beatrice noted how in sync they seemed to be. Most striking was that Caelan included Ella in the decision-making, listening to her opinions.

Her father and brothers never included her mother, Isobel, or her in any conversation dealing with clan matters. Most of the time, they found out things through what was overheard. She found it refreshing that the Ross men seemed to respect and not undervalue a woman's worth and intelligence.

As soon as she ate her fill, her eyes began drooping. "I will speak to my sister upon her arrival. For now, I must get some rest. I barely slept a wink last night." Beatrice pushed back from the table.

As soon as she stepped out into the corridor, Duncan walked out. "I will be returning to my home. If ye need anything, ye can send a guard."

"I am sure not to need ye for anything," Beatrice replied. "Thank ye for escorting me back. I should have told the truth from the moment we returned." She let out a sigh. "It always comes out in the end, does it not?"

There was a slight twitch to the corners of his mouth and for a moment, she thought he'd smile. "It does indeed."

"I am sure my sister will convince Darach to the lack of impropriety and nothing will come of this entire thing." She placed a hand on his forearm. "Thank ye for everything. I am not sure what would have happened if I had been caught in the storm alone. I apologize once again for the taking of yer time my impetuous nature caused."

His gaze met hers. It was as if he was going to say something but was not sure of the words. Then he nodded and returned into the dining room.

"He is the most interesting man," Beatrice said out loud as she made her way back to her bedchamber.

The same lad who'd given Ella the note sat alone at a table. Too engrossed in the platter laden with food that sat before him, he didn't notice her walking past. Beatrice smiled widely as she hurried up the stairs.

She'd have to ask Ella about the young lad's parents. He seemed very young to be walking from the village to the keep alone.

Once inside the bedchamber, sleep evaded, and she went to the window to look out to the scenery below. The day was shaping up to be sunny, which was good since Duncan would be riding home.

In the distance, more than the usual number of birlinns arrived at the shore and her heart quickened. Did it mean visitors had arrived? Or perhaps her sister and the laird returned. She leaned forward squinting while attempting to see clearer.

Her breath caught. Why had no messenger arrived with news? Or perhaps they were downstairs now.

Worst case, it would be her mother visiting. But as only two days had passed since Duncan's return from North Uist, it wasn't her. It couldn't be.

Frozen to the spot, she continued watching as several bìrlinns were brought to the shore. People began climbing down and soon a man on horseback galloped toward the keep.

She let out a long breath and squeezed her eyes shut. The laird and her sister had returned.

If the messenger arrived before Duncan left, then he would remain to await their arrival. Of course, even if he had ridden off, surely, he would see the bìrlinns arriving and turn around.

Why hadn't she stayed at the keep and waited for Duncan to come as he'd planned? If only she'd waited until then to speak to him about the interchange with her mother.

She prayed that the travelers would need rest and not have the energy to speak to her or the others right away.

Her maid, Orla, hurried in. "Do ye require anything? It seems yer sister and her husband have returned."

"How do ye know?"

Orla pointed to the ceiling. "Guards saw them arriving, several men and a carriage were immediately dispatched. It was just announced to the household. It is quite mad down-stairs; everyone is ensuring the home is perfect for their entrance."

Beatrice looked down at her dress. It was nice and looked to be in good order. She lowered to a stool in front of a mirror. "Would ye please brush out my hair and braid it?"

As the maid began doing her hair, Beatrice formulated

what to say to her sister. No doubt as soon as Darach arrived, he, Caelan, and Duncan would steal away to the study to discuss clan matters.

She and Ella would greet the women with food and something to drink.

Moments later, she hurried to the kitchen where she found Ella directing that food be taken to the family dining room and also to the study.

"Ye must have heard the news." Ella barely spared her a glance before turning to a maid. "Hurry go out and find some flowers for the dining table."

Ella returned her attention to Beatrice. "We should go to the front and wait. They will be arriving within moments.

Together they went through the great hall to the front entrance.

"Where is Caelan?" Beatrice asked looking around.

"I am sure he rode off to greet Darach and ensure protection was provided if it was needed."

It was not much longer before the first of the guards rode through the gates, followed by a carriage and then finally the Ross men on horseback.

As soon as the carriage stopped, the door was opened by a guardsman. Isobel, followed by Lady Mariel and lastly Annis, Isobel's maid, exited.

Beatrice rushed to her sister genuinely excited to see her. "I am so happy ye are back," she exclaimed and hugged Isobel who grinned widely.

"I am glad to find ye well, sister," Isobel replied looking her over. "I was afraid of harm befalling ye and having to explain to Mother that I left ye alone."

A reassuring smile took effort, but Beatrice managed it, and once again hugged her sister as it wavered. "Ye look well. I expected to find ye tired."

"Nonsense," Lady Mariel said. "We slept most of the trip here. The only thing we are right now is very hungry."

As they went inside, Beatrice looked over her shoulder to find that the Ross men were not talking to each other, but each of them doing other things. Darach was instructing servants to see about the luggage, Caelan spoke to a man who'd hurried to him as if seeking some sort of information, while Duncan, who'd obviously turned around, stood with his arms crossed watching his brothers.

He glanced over at her and met her gaze with his own unwavering one. The message seemed clear to her. She was not to worry.

Easy for him to say.

"What?" Isobel asked and Beatrice realized she'd muttered out loud.

"Nothing important. Food should be set out. Ye will enjoy what cook made. It smelled delicious when I was in the kitchen just moments ago."

Once they were settled in the dining room, Isobel ate with gusto, oblivious to the suddenly heavy air.

Lady Mariel ate but kept looking at Ella with a curious expression.

"What happened?" Lady Mariel asked, looking from Beatrice to Ella. "Caelan and Duncan seemed to find interest in every surrounding, not meeting my gaze. I know when they are hiding something."

"Nothing horrible," Ella said and looked at Beatrice who

sat across the table from her. "Ye should tell them."

"What did ye do?" Isobel asked, her eyes wide. "If ye got into trouble while I was gone, Mother and Father will be even more displeased than they are now. Ye were supposed to have returned home by now."

The best way to formulate it would be to point out the good things first. "I went to Duncan and Caelan's home to speak to Duncan about that very subject. I wished to ascertain how Mother was after receiving my letter asking to remain here for an additional time."

Isobel lifted an eyebrow but remained silent.

Lady Mariel was not as patient. "Please continue, lass."

"The storm hit when I was heading back. I had to find refuge from it and was gone until this very morning. But as ye can see, I am uninjured and have not sneezed once."

"Ye rode there and back alone?" Isobel gawked at her, her spoon in midair as an incredulous expression spread across her pretty face. "Oh my goodness, Beatrice, how could ye?"

"She rode there alone, but Duncan escorted her back," Ella, ever helpful, added. "Thank goodness, she may have caught her death out there. The storm was horrible…"

"We are aware Ella," Lady Mariel snapped. "We had to delay our departure because of it."

There was a long moment of silence as both Isobel and Lady Mariel absorbed the information. For a moment, Beatrice felt relief. Other than a strong scolding, it would be the end of it.

"Ye must marry," Isobel proclaimed. "Quickly before news of this spreads."

"I am sure no one will know." Beatrice mentally calculated

how many people did know.

Lady Mariel frowned. "Ella, who all knows?"

"The staff here all searched for her. Guards reported she rode out towards the village. Two were sent out, but the storm caused them to return. The entire household saw her and Duncan arrive together this morning."

With slow deliberate moves, Lady Mariel lifted a cup to her lips and took a drink. Beatrice didn't dare point out it was her cup that she drank from. Instead, she did her best to keep her galloping heart from bursting out of her chest.

"I am sure there is another solution. Marriage is extreme," Beatrice said to the room at large. "Nothing happened. He was a gentleman."

"Ye should be quiet and let us think," Isobel scolded. "I cannot believe ye would do something so rash. Even for ye, I cannot fathom why ye would consider it a good idea to ride out alone to a man's home."

"My son cannot marry. He is not going to marry ye, Beatrice." Lady Mariel met Ella's gaze. "We must find another solution."

Isobel shook her head. "There is no other solution. Ye do not know my brothers. Upon hearing of what happened, it is not my father who will be enraged. Evander and Padraig will not accept any other solution than marriage.

"I understand," Lady Mariel said. "If it were another of my sons, I would not hesitate to demand they marry."

"What are ye saying?" Beatrice asked more out of curiosity than feeling slighted. She had no desire to marry. Admittedly, if she did have to marry a Ross, Duncan would be her first choice. That said, she wondered why Lady Mariel was so against it.

Ella bit her bottom lip in thought. "What if she marries Stuart? He would agree when presented with… the situation."

"Would ye please explain to me, why he will not do it?" Isobel demanded, her expression stern. "If anyone marries Beatrice, it will have to be Duncan."

Just then Darach walked into the room. The large blond man made Beatrice shudder. Something about her sister's husband gave her pause. Perhaps it was the air of authority that made her cautious.

Despite the fact Isobel loved him dearly and he treated her sister well, Beatrice had yet to warm up to the man. Perhaps it was that he eyed her with the expression of someone who thought her daft.

To be fair her current actions did not exactly paint the picture of someone who thought things through.

"Everyone to my study. There is much to discuss."

With a nod, Lady Mariel stood, and seeing Beatrice's bottom lip quiver, she took her arm. "There, there, dear. All will be well. Do not fret."

Her sister was not as kind.

"She should definitely fret."

CHAPTER SIX

DUNCAN STOOD WITH his back to the wall, arms crossed, and legs shoulder width apart. Always the opposite, Caelan sat in a chair, his right ankle across the opposite knee, and a glass of whiskey in hand. He looked every bit a man of leisure.

Sometimes, he envied the pampered life Caelan had lived. He'd been sent away to boarding school, in the lowlands, by his mother. Had spent a long part of his youth in England, where he'd learned mathematics and other frivolous things. Upon his return to the highlands, he'd been ensconced in the large home where they both lived now.

Seeming to sense his regard, his brother met his gaze. "Do not worry yerself. This will be sorted out without ye having to marry."

Marriage. The one thing he never thought to be a weapon that could be yielded against him. He never dared to consider a lifetime partnership with a woman. The very idea of marriage was the reason he never attended weddings, nor had he ever been in a relationship.

It was not that he detested the idea. It was more that someone like him could never be a good husband.

Just then Darach returned, and with him, his sister, his mother, Isobel, and finally a red-nosed Beatrice.

His mother gave him a worried smile and came to him. She placed a hand on his arm and leaned into him. When he hugged her, it was apparent she wanted to soothe him. "Ye need to cut yer hair," she teased when he pushed his shoulder-length hair back.

Darach looked to the women seated. "Duncan cannot marry ye, Miss Beatrice."

A worried gaze met his for a fleeting moment before Beatrice looked to his brother. "I do not wish to marry anyone."

"That choice is not an option," his brother stated. "Ye will marry Caelan instead."

His usually calm brother choked on the whiskey and began coughing. Ella hit his back until he shook his head. By the time he spoke, his face was red.

"Why me?"

Beatrice gawked at Caelan. "Why do ye act as if it were a punishment worse than death?"

"Because I am not one to be ordered to marry," Caelan retorted. "Miss Beatrice, no offense, but I do not wish to marry ye."

"And I have no desire to marry a dandy like ye."

"Dandy?" Caelan's eyes rounded. "What makes ye think…"

"Stop," Darach ordered. "There is no other solution. Duncan cannot marry and if the Macdonald's hear of this, they will demand marriage. If Beatrice is already married, then it will soothe things."

"What about Stuart or Gideon? Both are more than able to fulfill this … this … situation," Caelan pointed out.

"What about what I want?" Beatrice stood and stomped

her foot. Fury blazed from her eyes as she looked at every person in the room, including him.

"I do not care what any of ye think. I will return home immediately and handle the situation myself."

She whirled to face him, her blue eyes blazing. "How dare ye not wish to marry me. I thought ye a man of honor. I understand not wishing to be forced; however, ye could have at least stood up for me. Convinced them nothing happened. Tell them ye and I are not suitable. But do not sir, just state: ye cannot marry me."

She spun and stormed from the room.

"I like her," Darach said looking at him. "A misfortune ye cannot marry her."

DUNCAN WALKED INTO the parlor and found Beatrice staring blankly at the view of the sea below them. By her furrowed brow and the tightness of her lips, he knew she remained furious. It was not the time perhaps to point out that everything could have been avoided if she'd remained there and waited for him to come.

It was stupid to try to reason with a woman, Duncan considered. He'd never argued with his mother or sister, or any woman for that matter. Most of the time if one grew angry with him, he would walk away or remain quiet until they gave up.

When Beatrice turned to him, her eyes widened. It as if she'd expected to find someone else. Perhaps her sister.

"What is it?" she asked in a tight voice. "If ye do not have a solution, I suggest ye leave me be as I struggle to come up with one."

"I do not wish to insult ye by refusing to marry ye. It has nothing to do with…"

When she made a slashing motion with her hand, he stopped talking. The beauty neared and circled him.

"Are ye married already?"

He shook his head.

Beatrice came back to stand in front of him, her gaze lowering down the length of his body. "Not fully able to fulfill yer obligations as a husband?"

Duncan cleared his throat. "That is not the reason."

Her eyes narrowed. "What is so horrible about ye then?"

The fact she used the word horrible was apt. What he harbored inside was indeed horrible. He took a breath. "Darach and Isobel will speak to ye about it. It is best that I do not."

Beatrice placed a hand on his arm to stop him from leaving. Her lovely eyes lifted to his. Upon their gazes clashing, Duncan felt a kinship with her and considered that he should marry her, and all consequences be damned. The thought of her with either Caelan or Stuart made his blood boil.

"I do not know what is wrong. In a way, it probably is not my secret to know. However, I have caused ye trouble and for that, I beg that ye forgive me."

The urge to pull her close and comfort her was strong, but Duncan managed to keep his arms against his sides. "Ye have nothing to apologize for."

"It seems I have learned a valuable lesson. My rashness causes problems for others and I should have known better. I am no longer a young lass that can act without thinking."

Her expression changed and he knew she'd come up with an idea. When she slid a gaze to the view outside, he inhaled sharply. "I hope ye do not plan to go on a sea voyage alone. If the trek to my house was dangerous, that would be perilous."

"I am not going anywhere," she quipped. "However, I do have a brilliant idea." When her lips curved, for the first time in his life, Duncan wished he could see it every day.

Without thought, he took her face and pressed his lips to hers.

Realizing what he did, Duncan pushed away abruptly with so much force Beatrice stumbled backward.

Both of them wide-eyed stood facing each other for a long moment.

"I-I…" he stuttered, unsure what to say after having done something so impulsive.

"First ye see me bereft of clothing and now ye kiss me. What is next?" Beatrice huffed, crossing her arms.

"Why did he see ye with no clothing on?" Isobel's voice sounded behind him.

Duncan closed his eyes. The day had just gotten worse.

When he opened them, Beatrice was gone, she'd rounded him to go to her sister. "Ye should not be lurking about eavesdropping."

"Did ye not think that small detail should have been disclosed?"

"He did not do it on purpose. I thought he was gone when I was naked."

Isobel glowered at Duncan. "So ye were undressed as well?"

"Goodness." Beatrice let out an annoyed breath. "We were soaked, had to remove our clothes to dry them or catch our death. He did not see me undress."

"Ye just said he saw ye bereft of clothes."

"Aye, when I was dressing, I thought him gone. My fault entirely to have removed the plaid without noticing he was there."

Isobel sized him up. "Duncan is a huge man, how could ye not notice he was in the room?"

"I had just woken up. I thought he'd slipped away while I slept."

It was difficult to keep up with the discussion between the sisters. Duncan found himself looking from one to the other, not needing to speak as they seemed to have forgotten he stood there.

Just then his mother walked in. "Excuse us, please ladies. I must speak to my son."

As the sisters walked away, Isobel insisted Beatrice retell what happened from the beginning.

HIS MOTHER MOTIONED for Duncan to sit and he lowered to a chair opposite her. Of all the rooms at the keep, the family parlor was his favorite. Keep Ross was over three hundred years old, and his family had made many changes. One of them was to tear down walls and construct a large room for family gatherings other than the great hall. Here in the parlor, the drapes were routinely pulled back to allow the sunshine in.

There were seating areas, shelves laden with books, and several pieces of furniture that reminded him of his childhood. During his father's constant absences, he and his siblings spent many a day in that room, either playing as children or as young men discussing what they considered to be items of dire importance.

His mother had assured them a good life and for it, he'd be forever thankful.

Now her expression was serious. The questions she was going to ask were difficult, but he understood.

"Tell me why ye think ye should never marry? Yer anger can be controlled, ye can remove yerself to another room or go outside." Her gaze was warm, while at the same time cautious.

Duncan shook his head. "I cannot marry. My body…a woman will recoil in horror if they see all the damage."

"The right woman will see past the scars son. I have not seen ye or heard of ye having any kind of issues in a long time."

He'd not kept count. In truth, it had been a long time since he'd become lost in the past. Even when Darach had been taken by a rival laird, he'd kept control.

"It has been a long time. I do things to keep my mind busy."

"Is this longer than usual?"

Duncan did not want to think or discuss something that would not change his mind. "I suppose."

"I must insist that ye consider marriage to Beatrice. She seems taken with ye, the first woman I've ever known to not be intimidated by ye," his mother said.

"Mother, I cannot marry…"

Lady Mariel shook her head. "Oh, Duncan. It is ye that is holding yerself back. Not the scars or the anger. Ye are afraid and I understand. But ye are letting it hold ye back from life. Yer father is dead, and the past is gone. We must move on."

Duncan shrugged. "I'm sorry Mother. I will not change my mind."

There was resignation in his mother's eyes. This was not the first time they'd had this conversation. "I think it is best that I speak to Beatrice, so she understands this is not a slight on our part."

The tightness in his chest was something he'd not felt in a long time. Grief over the fact he'd lost his life a long time ago. A part of him was dead, and although he went through the motions of living, his soul remained empty.

"I wish…" his mother began, but then hugged him instead. "Go see about getting a good meal before heading home."

"I have a cook Mother."

"Ye do not have Greer." She smiled knowing the cook had a soft spot for him.

HEADING HOME, DUNCAN allowed the horse to meander and take its time. There was nothing waiting for him back at the house other than the wall and time alone.

He happened upon a man standing on the side of the road, next to a lopsided wagon. When Duncan neared, the man shook his head and said, "Wheel broke."

"Ye can unhitch yer horse and ride to Keep Ross, they will help ye." Duncan studied the wagon in which sat a pair of young children. Clean and well-fed, they looked up at him with curiosity.

"Aye, I was about to take the bairns and do just that." He studied Duncan for a moment. "Ye are a Ross are ye not?"

"I am Duncan Ross," he replied.

"I am to see yer brother about finding my wife," the man

said, then lowered his voice. "Took off on myself and the bairns again. Light-skirts she is."

From the look of the man, he was caring, but perhaps a bit weak. If it were Duncan, he'd not go after the woman. "Why do ye want her back?"

"Look after the bairns. I work all day, have fifty head of sheep. Someone needs to keep them."

Duncan scratched his head. "Ask my brother to help ye find a nursemaid who will work for little money in exchange for a roof over her head."

It was obvious the man had not considered another option by the change in his expression from morose to excited. "Why didn't I think of that?"

"I do not know." Duncan maneuvered his horse so he could look to the children again. He plucked two coins from his purse and handed one to each of them.

Once on the road again, he couldn't help but wonder how a mother could abandon her bairns. From the looks of the children, they were well-behaved and bonnie. Perhaps it was her husband's weakness, he concluded.

The hair on the nape of his head lifted and he began scanning the surroundings. He was almost home, passing a field with scattered cusps of trees. The sensation of someone watching him became stronger, the closer he got home.

If someone was about, they hid well because he did not see anything amiss. Once arriving at the stables, Creagh, the stablemaster hurried out and took the horse to be looked after.

Duncan caught up with the man. "Have ye seen anyone about today?"

The man scratched his head. "Strange ye should ask. Earlier today, I saw a horseman riding away. It was as if he'd come near but decided not to stop."

"What did he look like?"

"Could not see clearly, he was a ways off. Only thing was his shoulders were off, his right much lower than the left."

The uneasy feeling followed Duncan as he went inside. He paced in the parlor considering who the person was.

It was rare that they had visitors and it was always someone of Caelan's acquaintance who came to relive old times. Often the men who came would only remain a day or two, drinking and talking until late in the night. Sometimes, they'd bring women to spend time with. Other times, they'd go into town to the tavern.

He felt more at ease and considering that perhaps the man who'd come near had met someone who'd informed him Caelan was not in residence.

"Do ye require anything, Mister Duncan?" Gara stood at the doorway, she and Firtha, the other servant, knew better than to approach him directly or go into a room where he was. They'd been witnesses to his darker side and despite it, had remained.

"Nay, I ate before leaving Dún Láidir. I will have last meal and that is all."

He walked back out and directly to the stone wall. While lifting each stone, he pictured Beatrice and her reaction to learning about his past. The muscles of his arms quivered as he lifted another heavy stone to place it atop the wall. Once in place, he leaned on the wall for a moment to catch his breath and then bent to get the next one.

CHAPTER SEVEN

L ADY MARIEL WAITED for the maid to leave the sitting room before speaking. Beatrice almost told her not to by the pain etched on her face.

"This is a story every mother hopes never to have to tell," she began. "To know the horrors my son suffered can never stop hurting my heart."

Isobel leaned to the woman and took her hand. "Ye do not have to tell us. If it is something so horrible that it keeps Duncan from marriage, yer word is enough."

"I agree," Beatrice added. "We can find another solution to the situation. Even if it comes to me having to marry another of yer sons. Although I do wish to make clear, is not the option I prefer."

Her lips curved as Lady Mariel met Beatrice's gaze. "Ye would make a fine wife for Duncan. But he is damaged and fears intimacy."

After a moment, she began to talk.

The grey skies did not promise an easy voyage and Duncan looked to his father, expecting him to call off the trip. He dared not say anything, else be backhanded in front of the others present.

They were to go to the shore of Skye to meet with a

ship. According to his father, there was to be a valuable shipment and he would be one of the first to purchase items that would be resold for a fortune.

Two men had come in the cloak of darkness to inform his father about it, and now they were set to go and meet the captain of the ship.

Once onboard the birlinn, the sea tossed it this way and that. The vessel tipping so far sideways, Duncan was sure he'd fall into the deep water.

His father ignored him the entire time, excitedly speaking to the men about the purchase. With only four guards, Duncan wondered about the wisdom of going so far with virtual strangers.

By the time they arrived ashore it was hours later, and Duncan was so exhausted he could barely stand.

"Come along," his father said grabbing him by the nape. "Do not dawdle. I brought ye to learn the ways of commerce. As second born, ye must have a trade. Do not make me regret it."

Silently, he followed his father along the planks of the seaside village until they met with yet another set of men.

Duncan listened as his father argued prices and the amount he was willing to purchase at said price. It came to a point during an argument that the guards had to intercede to keep the men from hitting Laird Ross.

Finally, an agreement was reached, and they were escorted to a nondescript house. Once inside there were piles of goods spread out in the large main room.

His father's eyes grew wide, and Duncan recognized the look of greed. Often his father had the same look upon seeing a woman he'd not noticed before, or when looking to acquire a new horse for the stables.

This time, however, the look was more intense.

"How much for that?" He pointed to neatly stacked fabrics. "I have never seen such colors."

If not for the unsettling appearance of the sellers, Duncan would have laughed at the thought of his father selling merchandise, like a common peddler.

"They are not for sale," a man replied. "They are already sold."

"What of that?" His father then pointed to sacks. "What is it?"

"Sugar," the same man said.

"I will take it."

They began to haggle. The entire trip was to Duncan a waste of time. His father would purchase the costly items and probably not resell them but keep them for himself. Not that Duncan cared one way or the other. He was not learning anything.

His father and the merchant both turned to him at the same time. There seemed to be some sort of silent communication. Instantly, Duncan felt ill at ease and took a step toward the door.

Just then the pressure of a hand on his shoulder made him turn. One of the vendors motioned for him to follow. "We have other items for sale. Ye may wish to purchase one before yer father does."

When he turned to his father, he waved him away. The expression of greed now joined with a curve of lips.

He walked behind the man until reaching a room. The man pushed the curtains aside and shoved Duncan through the doorway and then came to stand next to him. "Yer choice. Yer father agreed to pay."

Women lay on pillows. Most of them barely dressed. Each of them took him in and Duncan felt himself shrink back. Women would not find a lanky boy of ten and four to be enticing, much less wish to lay with him.

He knew about this kind of purchase as his brother Darach and his friends often spoke about it. But he'd never seen it.

"I do not wish to purchase anything," he said and turned on his heel.

Just outside the doorway, two large men stood with arms crossed. The man who'd shown Duncan the room shrank back. "What do ye want?"

"Ye are payment for very exclusive merchandise."

There was an awkward silence, one of them holding Duncan by the arm. "Ye will come with us."

"M-my father has much coin. He is in the other room making large purchases. Allow me to return to him . . ."

One of the men huffed and continued to block the way out. "Ye should take advantage of what is presented. It may be the last time ye will have the opportunity."

Just then the doors opened and the merchant who'd been haggling with his father appeared. He looked Dun-

can over.

"I am sure he will fetch a fair price."

As Duncan went to scream for his father, one of the men who held hit him in the stomach. The large fist taking all his breath.

The merchant narrowed his eyes at Duncan. "Take him out the back. Keep him silent, so as not to scare away other customers."

While being dragged out, Duncan struggled with all his might. Kicking, biting, and swinging his fists.

"Enough," one of the men said and punched him so hard, he could barely see for a few moments. The second hit sent him into darkness.

Upon coming to, the swaying of the ship and the smell of rotten fish turned Duncan's stomach. He was somewhere in the bowels of a large vessel. By the swaying, it was obvious they were not stationary, but moving at a fast speed.

Scrambling to his feet, he raced to the ladder and climbed up. On deck were several men, including one who'd been at the merchant's. The man turned to him, but then promptly ignored Duncan.

"Why am I here?" Duncan asked the man. "I wish to return home."

The man gave him an icy glare. "Ye are home."

Beatrice sat back. "He was taken at ten and four? How long was he gone?"

"Duncan was gone for ten years." Lady Mariel sighed. "He

returned broken and hollow. For a long time, barely speaking. Not used to large open spaces, he spent many days in a small bedchamber, only venturing out for short periods. It took years before he was able to have a somewhat normal life."

Tears pricked at her eyes and Beatrice allowed them to overflow down her cheeks. "I cannot fathom what happened to him all those years."

"He has told us a few of the experiences he went through. Many of them I cannot repeat. However, I will tell ye that he was tied to a post and whipped for simple misdeeds and left without food and water for days. As a result, my son has internal scars that may never heal."

Beatrice's heart broke for Duncan. She wished nothing more than to go to him and give him comfort. Although, he would probably not welcome it.

Her sister hugged Lady Mariel. "We should discuss Beatrice's situation more. There is time. Mother will not arrive anytime soon. Hopefully, we can come to a solution."

"I am going to rest. We should expect a lively last meal as the people wish to welcome Darach back," Lady Mariel said as she stood. Her warm gaze met Beatrice's "Do not worry yerself overly about this. It is not as bad as it seems."

Left with her sister, Beatrice became animated. "Surely ye do not think I should have to marry. I do not wish to anger our parents further. Being married when Mother arrives will send her to madness. I am sure she is already furious at my staying here longer."

"What explanation did ye give?"

Beatrice sucked in air. She'd forgotten about the excuse. "I told her I was being courted."

"By whom?" Isobel closed her eyes for a moment and opened them slowly. "I hope ye did not say Duncan."

When Beatrice didn't reply, her sister blew out a breath. "Beatrice, ye wish to be taken seriously. Ye claim to be mature, but yer actions are not those of someone who considers the consequences of their actions."

"Being impetuous does not make me immature," Beatrice shot back. "I admit to making mistakes and am doing what I can to come up with a way to not have to marry and not anger our parents at the same time. If ye would stop scolding and help, I am sure we can come up with a perfect solution."

"There is no other solution than for ye to marry. If not Duncan, then another of the brothers. Although displeased that ye do not marry a MacLeod, Mother at least will be pleased at a furthering of our attachment with Clan Ross. I am sure eventually she and Lady Mariel will be very glad for it."

It was left unsaid that Evander and their father would not be as thrilled. They needed a strong bond with the MacLeod. The man had two sons and one daughter, who was to be married off to another clan.

"Do ye wonder how clans would become united without marrying off their offspring?" Beatrice said while tapping a finger to her chin. "If ye ask me, they should not involve us. They should trade cattle or something."

"Beatrice, this is a very serious situation, we have to consider that we'd rather ye marry another of the Ross brothers than be forced into a life with a damaged man."

The word made her cringe. "Duncan is not damaged. That is a horrible thing to say." Beatrice blew out a breath. "Allow me a day, or two to consider things. I would like to speak to

Stuart. I'd rather marry him than Caelan, mainly because he lives with Duncan and that would be... awkward."

"Very well," Isobel replied and stood. Beatrice was glad when she left, and she was allowed time alone again.

There was a solution they'd not considered. She could travel back to North Uist immediately. Her family would not hear about any rumors if they remained there. With her back, her mother would have no reason to come there for a few months.

At the thought of leaving and not seeing Duncan again, she became sad. In truth, she was very attracted to him and despite Lady Mariel's revelations, Beatrice felt a kinship with him. Interesting since she'd never suffered any type of injustice and lived what one could call a sheltered life. However, something deep within called to him and she could only suppose it was that with him, she felt safe.

He'd kissed her. Perhaps it had been an impulse. Obviously, he'd been very shocked by his actions. Had he done to soothe her feelings and then realized it had the opposite effect? Whatever the reason, she wished it had lasted more than a second. In truth, it barely counted as a kiss.

Beatrice huffed and looked toward the window. How hard would it be to get him to kiss her again? Not because she wanted to force him into another awkward situation, but because the short interlude made her curious to know what his kisses would be like.

First, she packed all her clothes, and upon Orla entering, she instructed the maid to finish. "I will see about returning home in the morning. Ye should pack yer belongings as well."

"Does Lady Ross know?" Orla said referring to Isobel.

"Not yet, I will inform her as soon as she is rested. I do not wish to disturb her right now."

Once the packing was done, Beatrice went to find Ella.

She found her outside in the side garden looking off into the distance.

"What are ye doing looking so forlorn?" Beatrice asked.

"Do ye ever wonder what else there is to life?" Ella replied, her gaze still off into the distance. "I find myself growing weary of the same thing, day in and day out."

Beatrice took Ella's hand. "Come with me to North Uist. I have a grand idea. If I return immediately, my family will not learn of what happened. No knowledge, no forced marriage."

For a long moment, Ella studied her. "I agree. It is a grand idea. We must tell Mother at once."

"Allow them to rest. There is time. However, I do wish for ye to come with me. It will give ye opportunity to get away for a bit and to see different dull views."

Ella burst into laughter. "Ye are a delight, Beatrice. I would very much love to travel with ye. There is nothing holding me here, if I am to be honest. A season away would be nice."

LADY MARIEL FROWNED, turning from Ella to Beatrice. "The idea has merit. Although I hate to keep anything away from yer mother," she said pinning Beatrice with a pointed look.

"If ye do not come with us, then any blame will lay with me for not informing her," Ella said. "Mother, we cannot force either Beatrice or Stuart to marry because of a weather mishap."

"I will speak to Darach. If he agrees then ye both can travel immediately." Lady Mariel let out a sigh and gave Beatrice a warm look. "If Duncan could marry, ye would be a perfect match for him."

Her chest constricted at the thought of marriage to Duncan. He was so very perfect in every way. In her opinion at least.

"I would not protest to marrying him," Beatrice replied.

An astonished expression crossed both Lady Mariel and Ella's faces. Ella recovered first. "Ye really do care for him. That is so very endearing."

"He will be here tomorrow. Ye can inform him of yer departure," Lady Mariel told her with a warm smile. "I am sure he would like to know."

LAST MEAL WAS as expected. The great hall was filled with village people who came to see their laird and lady, and to partake of the feast. Musicians played lively tunes and people danced after they'd ate their fill.

Beatrice and Ella sat at a table with a visiting landowner and his wife. Despite her situation, Beatrice was enjoying the evening. More than anything, she loved seeing her sister seated at the high board stealing glances at her handsome husband.

The laird did the same, ever so often touching Isobel's hand or leaning into her ear to whisper. Her heart ached when considering she wanted the same—a love match.

However, it seemed it would not be her lot in life. Instead, she hoped to learn to care for the man her parents matched her with.

"Look," Ella whispered into her ear. "Duncan is here."

Across the room, Duncan walked along the perimeter of the room and sat at a table in a corner. A moment later, Stuart and Gideon joined him.

"I wonder why my brother returned so soon. He just left earlier."

Beatrice shrugged. "Perhaps he forgot something."

"It could be," Ella studied her brothers for a moment. "I have to know." She stood and hurried over to where her brothers were.

"I hear North Uist is beautiful this time of year," the woman at the table, whose name she'd forgotten, said.

Beatrice smiled. "It is. However, not as warm as it is here." She slid another look at the corner. The siblings continued talking, but it seemed not to be anything serious.

Finally, Ella returned. "He got word of a shipment and will be traveling north in two days. I informed him that ye and I wish to go."

"Oh," Beatrice looked back to where Duncan sat, "do ye think that is a good idea?"

"He will not be going to yer home. We will be traveling there alone with an escort of course."

Hopefully, it would not turn into yet another complication. Beatrice nodded and looked to her sister. "I must speak to Isobel."

Out of the corner of her eye, she saw Duncan slip out a doorway. Without a word, she stood and pretending interest in the dancers, slowly made her way out the same door.

Duncan stood with his back to the house. He peered up at the sky, his stance relaxed.

"I must speak to ye," Beatrice whispered and walked closer

until she stood beside him.

"What about?" Duncan replied, not looking at her.

"I-I am not sure how to express my regret for all of this."

When he turned to face her, she felt small and insignificant. He was so beautiful under the moonlight. The dark waves of his loosed hair framed his strong face and his two-toned eyes flashed with something that she could not identify.

He took a step closer, and Beatrice considered if she should turn and flee. It was not what she wanted to do, she wished to stand her ground and be closer to him.

"Beatrice, ye should go back inside," he said, his face just a breath away.

"And if I do not?" she replied breathlessly.

When his mouth covered hers, every ounce of her body filled with joy. Beatrice clung to his shoulders, kissing him back.

His arms surrounded her as the kiss intensified. He tilted his head, to deepen the kiss, their tongues entwining. She'd never been so thoroughly kissed and never had her body responded in the way it did in that moment.

Tingles ran down her arms and legs and she wanted to wrap herself around him.

Not wishing him to move away, Beatrice threaded her arms around his neck, not letting go when he broke the kiss. Instead of releasing him, she nuzzled her face into his neck pressing her lips to the pulse there.

Duncan moaned softly and ran his hands up and down her sides. Then he took her mouth again, this time lifting her off her feet. It was as if she floated in the air, only the night air and stars witnesses to the first time she'd felt so utterly undone.

The feel of his mouth on hers, his strong arms around her body, and the scent of him were intoxicating. She never wished it to stop.

"We must stop," he finally said in a ragged voice and lowered her to the ground. Her knees barely held her up, so Beatrice leaned on him and wrapped her arms around his waist.

"That was wonderful," she said smiling up at him. "We should do it again."

For the first time since meeting him, his lips curved, and he shook his head. "Ye are unlike any woman I've ever met."

"I will take it as a compliment."

"Go back inside, ye will be missed." He tried to dislodge her arms from around his waist. "Beatrice."

She looked at him. "Ye wish to marry me. I know it."

A frown marred his brow. "Go inside."

"Kiss me again and I will."

There was warmth in his gaze. "Ye are a vixen. Quite hard to resist." Their mouths met with a sense of desperation, the knowledge that it was in all probability the last time they would be alone.

Beatrice couldn't help the moan that escaped, and she raked her fingers through his hair pulling him closer. Their bodies pressed against each other's; she could not fathom another man feeling so perfect. He was so very strong. Moving his lips along hers, Duncan traced kisses to her jaw and down the side of her neck while she clung to him lost in the wonderful sensations.

"This is certainly not what I expected to walk out to," Lady Mariel exclaimed.

With a gasp, Beatrice pushed away from Duncan. She swayed and he steadied her.

"We were just…talking," Beatrice said pushing Duncan's hands away. "Is that not true?" She peered up at Duncan, who fought to keep his breathing controlled.

The door opened and Darach stepped through. His keen gaze locked first with Duncan and then moved to Beatrice, locking on her swollen lips.

"Ye will marry her," he said then turned on his heel and went back inside.

Beatrice didn't dare look at Duncan. Looking to Lady Mariel, she let out a breath. "May I have a word with Duncan. I promise to come inside promptly."

Duncan's mother looked to her son for a long moment. "I will be right inside. Hurry."

When she left, Duncan remained still as a statue, looking in the direction of the door. "I am sorry."

"Listen," Beatrice said tugging at his sleeve. "When ye travel in two days. Take me back to North Uist. My family will not know anything about what happened."

"My brother will insist we marry immediately. I know him."

"Oh." Beatrice scrambled to come up with another plan.

Duncan took her by the arms and waited for her to look at him. "I will marry ye and ye will remain here at the keep, with my family."

"What?" Beatrice shook her head. "We are to live separately?"

"It is for the best." He rounded her and walked toward the courtyard.

When she went inside, Lady Mariel was standing in the doorway, prepared to go out.

Beatrice gave her an apologetic look. "Every time I try to fix things, I only make them worse. Now he hates me."

"I am sure he felt quite the opposite," Lady Mariel said hugging Beatrice. "Now tell me what he said."

"That once we marry, I will remain here, and he will continue to live at the other house."

"We will see about that." Lady Mariel lifted Beatrice's chin. "Come, I am sure yer sister wishes to speak to ye."

"This has been the longest day," Beatrice said sagging. "I want to go to bed and begin the day anew."

CHAPTER EIGHT

DUNCAN ENTERED HIS brother's study. "Ye know full well I will never marry. Why did ye make that statement."

"Because it is obvious there is something between ye and her. Already she has been compromised. Someone else may have spied ye and her just now." Darach met his gaze. "Sit down."

His pulse raced as the reality of what was about to happen settled within. His brother would not relent in this and Duncan did not blame him. Their mother had walked in on what could only be described as a passionate interlude.

"Why do ye fight the idea of a future with a wife and family so much?" Darach asked while pouring whiskey into two glasses. He handed one to Duncan and sat across from him. "Tell me."

Duncan blew out a breath. "There are many reasons."

"He is a scared virgin," Stuart said strolling in and went straight to the sideboard to get himself a drink. "We can get ye a woman to practice with."

"I am not a virgin," Duncan said staring daggers at their younger brother. Stuart could be his twin, with the same dark hair, and strong jaw. However, Stuart's eyes were both hazel and he was built like the archer that he was, with slender hips, and strong shoulders and arms.

"When were ye with a woman last?" Darach asked, obviously believing Stuart's statement.

"Before my entire body was covered in scars. Before a woman would scream in horror at the sight of me naked." He set his jaw waiting for Stuart to make another humorous remark. He was prepared to punch him.

Instead, his younger brother shook his head. "Ye should not allow that to hold ye back. There are ways to enjoy lovemaking without having to remove all yer clothing."

"I am aware," Duncan retorted and swallowed down the contents of his glass. "I prefer not to."

Darach looked at him. "Yer chest is not as scarred as yer back. When a woman is under ye or if she straddles ye, she will not see it."

It was both embarrassing and endearing that his brothers began coming up with ways for him to enjoy bedsport without revealing his marred body.

"Ye cannot keep from marrying Miss Beatrice. She is beautiful and obviously taken with ye," Stuart added. "Over time, ye can divulge more of yerself. Already she is aware of what happened to ye, that ye were stolen away when young."

Duncan was sure once she saw what he looked like she would want nothing to do with him. It would be her choice and he would allow it. There would be no blame or resentment on his part because he already understood that most people would be repulsed at seeing evidence of torture.

"It isn't fair to her. She deserves a husband to be proud of."

"Let her decide, brother. I do believe she has a good heart," Darach said. "The marriage will take place tomorrow."

"I have to meet with the ship captain. We cannot allow

him to sell the goods to someone else."

Darach shook his head. "Stuart can go."

"Stuart gets sick just looking at the sea," Duncan argued. "It should be me."

"I will go," Stuart said, his face already seeming to turn green at the thought.

"I will speak to Ewan, he and ye can go. Catriona is well enough to be left alone now. Ella or Mother can go see about her while Ewan is gone," Darach said to Stuart.

Stuart walked out, but Darach motioned for Duncan to stay. "I want ye to be happy; however, at the same time, I will insist ye consummate the marriage. Do not cross me on this. If ye do as we say, she will not see ye."

"Women wish to touch while making love. I cannot control that."

Darach nodded. "Ye were so young when ye left. I cannot imagine what lovemaking was like for ye then. When making love to a woman, ye must kiss and caress her until she is ready for ye."

While Darach explained the mechanics of making love and instructing him on how to keep Beatrice from touching his back, Duncan listened intently. He wanted to know everything, to ensure Beatrice enjoyed her first time.

"There is something else," Darach said. "It will be like yer first time as well. Do not expect it to be perfect. Over time ye will both learn what the other enjoys most and where to touch and kiss to bring more pleasure."

"Thank ye," Duncan said and leaned back.

"If ye ever have any questions, come to me," Darach said and leaned forward to place a hand on Duncan's shoulder. "I will always be here for ye."

When he walked outside it was dark, and he looked up at the star-filled sky. When he was aboard one ship after another, usually tied up or laying on the deck too injured to move, he would often look up at the stars. It was the only constant in his life, the lighted night sky, the time when he would sleep and dream of home and the green fields of his homeland.

If ever there were days when he'd not been mistreated, he would climb up to the mast and imagined reaching up to grab a star.

"Duncan?"

He turned to find Isobel, his brother's wife. "How do ye feel?"

It was an interesting question. He would have thought she'd be with Beatrice doing much what Darach had. Explaining to her what to expect in the marriage bed.

"I am well." He met her gaze. "How is Beatrice?"

Isobel smiled. "She is fast asleep. We talked, but it has been a long day. I believe she is looking forward to tomorrow."

"My apologies for the way things happened."

"Do not apologize for the situation my sister put ye in. It is I who should apologize for my sister's actions. Now ye are to be forced into marriage and after yer life, I would hope that ye would have a say in something so important."

"I am not against marrying yer sister. To have her as a wife is a priceless gift. She deserves more than me."

Isobel's lips curved into a warm smile. "She has chosen ye. Beatrice is not the delicate creature some think. I believe she made a choice and did what she could to claim ye."

"Then I am a fortunate man," Duncan replied.

When left alone, once again he looked up to the skies. He'd had sexual relations after ten and four. However, he had not been a willing participant and it was something he never ever thought about.

IN THE SHADOWS, a figure skulked away, slipping further into the darkness, a soft chuckle swallowed by the sounds of the wind.

CHAPTER NINE

A T THE FIRST sign of sunlight, Beatrice got out of bed and hurried to the window. She hoped for a sunny day as she wished to pick flowers for her hair and a bouquet. Awake since before dawn, she'd been planning mentally what to wear and how to do her hair.

Despite that the marriage was to be rushed, she was excited at the prospect of marrying Duncan. Not only was he the most handsome man she'd ever met, but the one man who drove her mindless with passion.

His kisses alone were better than she could have imagined. And the feel of his strong body against hers was like a fairy tale.

The only worry was that he would be angry or disappointed in having to marry her. Beatrice turned from the window and considered seeking him out. She had to know how he felt. If he was against the marriage, she would convince him to take her directly to a bìrlinn and send her home. They would have to be sneaky about it, but it could be done.

After wrapping herself in a robe, she slipped on soft slippers and went out the door. Thankfully the corridor was empty. It was still too early for anyone to be up. She imagined Greer and the kitchen maids were preparing for their day, but everyone else would be asleep.

The only problem was that she had no idea where Duncan's bedchamber was. She went to a door and opened it just enough to peek in. Gideon was splayed across his bed, fully dressed.

Then she walked past Ella's bedchamber and the one she knew was Stuarts and came to the last door at the end of the hall.

Cracking the door just enough, she peeked in.

Whoever lay on the bed had his back to the door and was fast asleep. Immediately she knew it was Duncan.

There were deep cuts and long scars crisscrossing his wide back. Deep pits caused by some sort of torture weapon trailed down his right side to below the edge of the blanket. Raised scars intersected with the others not just on his back, but also the backs of his arms.

Her horrified gaze followed each trail, unable to move as she took in the sight. How he must have suffered. There wasn't an inch of his back that was left unmarred.

Beatrice wanted to cry at the thought of all the pain he'd gone through. Somehow, she managed to swallow down the urge to make any sound.

Duncan could not know what she'd seen. It would have to be on his terms that he allowed her to see his body.

Tears trickled down her face as she closed the door gently and hurried back to her bedchamber. Once inside, she went to a chair and sat down, so she could lean forward and draw deep breaths.

How had he withstood it? It had to have been many whippings to have made the huge, raised scars. From the back of his neck to his waist, there was not one inch left untouched. There had to have been countless days and nights, he must have lay in agony without anyone to care for him.

She wondered if any of his family had seen it. Probably. And now it made sense, why they were all so protective of him. To expose him to rejection by a wife would be heartbreaking.

"Thank goodness he has me," Beatrice whispered to the empty room as she wiped away tears. "My poor, Duncan."

It was almost an hour later that Isobel entered her bed-chamber, behind her their maids, Annis and Orla, carried trays so that she and Isobel could have first meal there.

"I thought we'd go to Lady Mariel's sitting room," Beatrice said watching as the plates and food were set up.

Isobel shook her head. "No time. The wedding is to be this morning. The vicar has to attend to a burial this afternoon in a village far from here."

"It is a good day when one comes before a dead man," Beatrice quipped despite the butterflies in her stomach. "Isobel?"

"Aye?"

"If we are to be married first thing, what about the bedding? It will be this night will it not?"

"Do not fret," Isobel replied patting her shoulder. "Ye will have the entire day to spend with Duncan. Perhaps go to his house. Or ye could remain here. It will be up to ye both to decide."

"He has only two women as staff." Beatrice looked to Orla. "Will ye come with me?'

"Aye, of course I will," the young woman replied with a bright smile. Beatrice liked Orla, a pretty lass with bright green eyes and reddish hair. She had just enough of a sprinkling of freckles across her nose that they added to her charm.

"Good," Beatrice said. "Since I am packed already, then I think it will be best for us to remove ourselves to the other estate. Getting unpacked and settled will help distract me."

"Do ye not think planning time alone with Duncan should take precedence over unpacking?" Isobel asked with a grin.

Once again, the butterflies took flight. "Ye are right, of course. That is what I should do. Plan a picnic, or go for a walk…"

"I am sure ye will spend a wonderful day, no matter what ye decide to do."

Once they finished eating, a bath was brought. Unfortunately, there was little time to linger, so she washed up and allowed Annis and Orla to help her dress.

She chose a pale lavender dress that she knew enhanced the color of her eyes. Once the dress was on, it felt as if the rest of the preparations were done to someone else and she was a mere spectator. Absent from her body, she could barely hear anything said, the only sounds were her breathing and the gentle thuds of her heart. In her mind, she pictured Duncan's back, the scarring, both deep and raised. The expanse of his back and how horribly marred it was.

No one should ever be mistreated in such a terrible manner and yet the man she was to marry had endured more than most humans.

Despite what he'd been through, he remained gentle with her, forgiving and caring. Duncan represented security and calmness and as unfathomable as it was, Beatrice knew deep in her heart they were meant for one another.

Finally, Lady Mariel came to the door and told them it was

time. When she saw Beatrice, her face softened. "Ye are a beautiful bride dear. My only regret is that Aileen is not here to see ye."

"She will be sad," Isobel said. "But we will plan a wedding celebration when she arrives."

As she made her way to the door, her sister took her arm. "A messenger will be dispatched to inform our parents of the wedding and to let them know festivities are planned for when they arrive."

"Good," Beatrice said and took a shaky breath. "I am about to be married. I can scarcely believe it."

THEY WENT DOWN the stairwell and turned to the left to a corridor that led to a small chapel. Inside people were already seated in the pews. The council members, Ewan, his wife Catriona, Stuart, and Gideon. There were a few staff members that she'd met and some villagers, she'd not met. Beatrice recognized the tavern owner and his wife, whom she'd purchased items from at the village square.

Caelan was there as well, he was seated with a man she expected by his similar features to be his half-brother. Finally, when she looked to the front of the chapel, she lost her breath.

Dressed in Ross colors of green and black, Duncan wore the plaid wrapped around his waist and draped over his left shoulder. It was held in place with the clan crest. His hair was pulled back into a queue, and on his feet were leather boots.

Next to him dressed alike, was Darach, who'd brushed his hair back to wear it like Duncan. The brothers made a breathtaking picture, one light, one dark, both standing proud, with matching serious expressions.

Beatrice looked to Duncan until his eyes met hers and his face softened. It was the reassurance she needed to force her legs to continue moving toward him.

When she reached the front, they stood facing each other as the vicar began speaking.

The words spoken over them were pure and beautiful, each syllable seeming to pierce her skin until reaching into every part of her. A sigh escaped her when Duncan's eyes locked with hers and his strong voice repeated his portion of the vows. When it was her turn, Beatrice spoke in an even tone, hesitating only once to swallow as tears spilled down her cheeks. It was such a special moment, she did her best to convey to Duncan the depth of her feelings by not looking away as she spoke.

Once the vows were exchanged, the vicar allowed a kiss. Duncan pressed his lips to hers in a soft kiss that made her smile. He looked to be at peace, not upset at all over the forced marriage and for that Beatrice was thankful.

As they walked out of the chapel, the people cheered. Once in the courtyard, those that had gathered clapped and called out congratulatory remarks.

Finally, they went back into the house where they were to toast to the marriage. According to Isobel, there were to be sweet cakes and meats for them to share with those attending.

Duncan took her elbow and guided her to the high board. Once she settled, he lowered next to her. There were pitchers of ale at every table, and everyone filled their cups.

Once it was accomplished, Darach stood and held his cup up.

"I wish ye both a good marriage and the blessing of many

bairns."

There were serious toasts and others that brought laughter as each brother stood and spoke. Lady Mariel was last, and she spoke wishing them happiness and insisted that she believed them to have been matched by God and therefore would have a good marriage.

Isobel could barely get the words out past her tears as she spoke for their family. "As representative of Clan Macdonald, I want to express how grateful we are for the connection of our clans, the strength Duncan and Beatrice's marriage brings to both of our families, and the peace this union ensures. I too am thankful that my sister and I will live near each other. And I know my father and mother will be forever grateful for Duncan's care of their daughter."

Once the toasts were complete, Beatrice accepted a handkerchief so she could wipe her wet face. Duncan leaned close to speak into her ear. "How do ye feel?"

"Nervous, happy. Very nervous." She met his gaze. "Ye?"

"The same," he admitted.

His answer surprised her, but she was grateful for his honesty. That a man such as him, a seasoned warrior would feel anxious about things made her feel closer to him.

The festivities continued for several hours until it was time for the midday meal where roast duck with succulent root vegetables, along with freshly baked bread were served.

Beatrice acknowledged that by the time they arrived at Duncan's home it would be late in the day.

"Are we to go to yer home after this?" she asked her new husband.

Duncan nodded. "Aye, yer sister informed me of yer family tradition of remaining close for fifteen days. I assume ye wish to continue it."

"I very much do," she answered honestly.

He did not reply, simply nodded to let her know he heard.

Despite the happy feelings, she wondered how long before he insisted she return to Keep Ross.

THE TRAVEL TO the other estate took less time than she remembered from her last trek there. Probably because, unlike her, the carriage driver knew the way. There were in one of the Ross carriages, pulled by two horses. Duncan's horse was tethered to the back of the carriage.

Orla rode up front on the bench next to the driver, to allow the newlyweds time alone. However, as soon as the carriage began moving Beatrice fell asleep with her head on Duncan's shoulder.

No sooner had she closed her eyes, did it seem he woke her to tell her they'd arrived.

Upon arriving, both of the maids stood outside to greet them. There were a couple of additional women standing beside them, obviously sent by Lady Mariel to help Beatrice settle. She planned to hire a chambermaid and perhaps a couple of lads to help with menial tasks once she had spoken to Duncan about it.

He assisted her from the coach and the housekeeper, and the other woman hurried forward. "I am Gara, milady," she said with a wide smile. "This is Firtha." She motioned to the woman beside her, who bobbed a curtsy.

"I am happy to see ye both again," Beatrice replied. "Although I did see ye last time I was here."

The woman looked to Duncan. "There's no need for additional help, the house is in perfect order. Firtha and I saw to it."

"My mother does not mean it as a slight, she wishes for Lady Beatrice to be settled without effort," Duncan replied with a soothing tone.

They went inside, Duncan guiding her to what she assumed would be their bedchamber. She'd not thought to ask if they would share one. Her parents had separate bedchambers, which made sense as her father needed extra space on the bed, to be comfortable.

The room they entered was large, with a four-poster bed, several rugs strewn about, and no décor on the walls. Other than a dressing table and a washstand, there were no other furnishings.

A trunk was pushed against one wall, where she assumed Duncan kept his clothes. This was definitely his bedchamber.

"Am I to sleep here from now on?" Beatrice asked, looking around the room already planning where a wardrobe would fit.

"This is my bedchamber, yers is adjacent. I thought it would be easier for ye to have yer own space." When he met her gaze, it was as if he were holding back something else he wanted to say.

The thought of not sharing a bedchamber had not occurred to her, especially since Isobel and Darach had slept in the same bed since they married. But she nodded in agreement. "May I see it please?"

He nodded and went to a door across from the bed. When he opened the door, it took effort. Duncan had to yank hard for it to open.

"Obviously it hasn't been used for a long time," Beatrice remarked dryly.

The bedchamber they entered was beautiful. Fresh bedding had been placed on the large bed and there was a throw tossed over a chair by the hearth to ensure whoever was there kept warm.

The drapes that framed the window were of a light fabric, more for aesthetics than practicality. There was a large wardrobe against one wall and next to it a paneled screen for private matters.

On the floor the rugs were thick and luxurious and on one wall was an embroidered tapestry with a scene of a woman at a fountain.

"Was this bedchamber always decorated like this?" Beatrice asked. "It is beautiful."

"I am not sure. Mother and my sister often come here and redo things. Though I do know, Mother slept in this chamber when she stayed the night. They probably sent items ahead for the servants to place here as well."

Upon the dressing table was a sealed letter sitting next to a beautiful looking glass. Beatrice did not make to open it, she would soon.

Her trunk and other items were already in the room. Beatrice turned to Duncan. "I will prepare for bed. Will ye come here to me?" Her voice trembled a little in anticipation of what was to happen between them.

"Aye, I will give ye some time." He looked at her for a long moment, once again as if he wished to say something, but instead let out a breath.

"Duncan?" Beatrice placed her hand on his forearm. When he met her gaze, she smiled. "I am fortunate to have ye for a husband."

He swallowed visibly, leaned forward, and placed a soft kiss on her lips. "It is I who do not deserve someone like ye."

Following his departure, she wondered why someone like him, from a prominent and wealthy family, would feel less than anyone. Perhaps there was more to his story than just the abduction and mistreatment he'd suffered over the years he was enslaved.

Over time, Beatrice would find out as much as she could and help him heal. It was obvious to her that he'd not made peace with his past yet.

For now, she had to learn to make the best out of the situation. Looking around the room she wondered how long before she would inform him that she did not believe in separate bedchambers in marriage.

It was nonsense in her opinion to be separated by a door that was so hard to open. If that wasn't a metaphor for trouble ahead, she wasn't sure what was.

Orla entered after knocking and helped Beatrice undress. The maid was giddy, talking nonstop about the bedchamber she'd been given. "Ye wouldna believe it, Lady Beatrice. Tis grand. I have my own room with a big bed and even a dressin' table."

"I am so happy to hear it Orla. Annis will be jealous when she comes to visit. Although her room at the keep is nice, it sounds like yers is grand."

"Oh, it tis."

Beatrice giggled when Orla attempted to tell her what to expect. The young woman had never been with a man, but she claimed to have caught her brothers in the act several times. "I tell ye, Lady Beatrice. The lass was yellin' but in a good way. Seemed to be havin' the time o' her life."

"Orla, when ye marry, I cannot wait to hear what happens on yer wedding night."

"I have no prospects yet, but I will find a kind man one day," Orla informed her.

Hair brushed out and wearing a white nightgown, Beatrice climbed on the bed to wait for Duncan. It was only a few moments later that he tugged the door open and walked in.

"I have to get the door fixed," he mumbled and then stopped in his tracks upon seeing her sitting up in bed, legs crossed. "What are ye doing? Are ye not supposed to be laying down?"

Beatrice shrugged. "I have no idea how I am expected to pose." She chuckled. "Will ye pour some honeyed mead for me. It will help with my nerves."

"Aye, of course." He poured mead into two small glasses and neared the bed. Once she took hers, he climbed onto the bed and leaned back on the headboard.

The liquid trailed down her throat immediately warming her insides. Although she felt a bit calmer, her stomach continued to flutter every time she looked to her husband.

He took the glass and slid from the bed. Then to her shock, he blew out every light in the room leaving them in darkness.

There wasn't even moonlight as she heard him fumble with his clothes.

"I cannot see anything," Beatrice complained.

"It is easier for me to sleep with no light in the room," Duncan replied.

Beatrice huffed. "We are not to sleep right away. We have to… well ye know."

"I am aware," he replied tightly.

She flopped back onto the bed to wait for him to join her. After her eyes adjusted Beatrice could track Duncan's movements. He undressed slowly as if measuring every movement. She wondered at his hesitation.

If he was as nervous as her, the consummation would be awkward. However, it had to be done and she expected once they got to know each other better, things would be easier. Finally, he joined her, his large body seeming to take the entire space. Beatrice turned on her side to face him.

"It is strange not to see ye clearly. Are ye sure we must have complete darkness?"

Instead of a reply, he touched her cheek and his mouth pressed on hers. Duncan pushed her onto her back while continuing to kiss her. His hand slipped under her nightgown and then slid up the outside of her left leg. Beatrice could not help but shiver at the intimate touch, her body hummed with expectation and at the same time, she was scared.

His breaking the kiss brought her attention back to him and she lifted her arms to allow him to remove her nightgown. She was completely bare, then again, so was he.

Duncan moved closer, but did not climb over her, instead, he continued to caress her body, his callused hands causing tingles of awareness.

Air left her lungs when he cupped her sex and Beatrice

gasped. It was unexpected, but at the same time, she had no idea what should happen.

His fingers slid up and down her center and she fought to remain still while biting her bottom lip to keep from making any untoward noises.

Seeming satisfied at whatever he did, Duncan came over her. "Put yer arms around my neck," he instructed.

Beatrice did as he said but could not think past the fact he pulled her legs apart and settled between them.

His breathing was harsh, fanning across her face as he fumbled with something. She expected it was what Isobel had informed her. That he would take his hardened sex and enter her.

At this point, she was so scared a tear escaped and she squeezed her eyes shut. It was not exactly the right thing because then all she could do now was feel and smell.

A part of him, she assumed his sex prodded between her legs. Then he pushed in. Despite his slow movements, it was uncomfortable and a bit painful to be stretched.

"Just do it please," Beatrice exclaimed when he hesitated. "I know the first time it will hurt, and I would rather it be over."

Duncan cleared his throat. "I am sorry." The first attempt to thrust in did nothing, his sex remained in the same place. "Ye are very small. I am not sure if this is right. To hurt ye like this."

Despite her efforts, she moaned at the rather invasive sensation. It was not exactly painful in that moment, if anything it was a bit comical. Beatrice pressed her lips together and forced herself to relax.

Duncan pushed in and this time, he filled her completely.

It was obvious when he tore past her maidenhead, but it wasn't terribly painful. Beatrice was too distracted at being completely joined with him.

He began moving, his hips lifting and lowering at first the pace was slow, but quickly he seemed to lose control.

When a hoarse groan erupted, Beatrice could only wonder what he felt. Although it wasn't completely horrible, she would not describe the experience as enjoyable.

He rolled onto his back and pulled her against his side. Under her ear his heart was beating frantically, his chest expanding with each sharp inhalation.

"How do ye feel?" He pressed a kiss to her temple.

Beatrice considered it. "I do not feel any different, like I expected."

"Ye did not enjoy it, did ye?"

"I did not hate it."

Duncan chuckled. "We will have to learn together. I want our bedsport to bring ye pleasure."

The statement was curious. "Ye are experienced are ye not?"

Her new husband was silent for a long moment. "No. I have not been with a woman, but twice and that was many years ago."

The news made Beatrice smile. "I am glad."

"Why? Most women prefer a man who knows what to do."

"I do not. We will learn together, and I think that will be more enjoyable." She lifted to her elbow. "Tell me what ye like when I do it."

Duncan exhaled. "What do ye plan to do?"

Without speaking, Beatrice leaned over him and pressed

her mouth to his. When his lips parted, she slid her tongue into Duncan's mouth, and he suckled at it.

Sliding her hand down the center of his chest, she hesitated at the soft hair atop where his sex was and made circles with her fingers.

Duncan's breath caught, a sign her touches were affecting him.

She then caressed his inner thighs, not quite comfortable touching any other part of him.

"What did ye think?"

"It was very enjoyable. Now ye." He pushed her onto her back but did not kiss her on the mouth. Instead, he pressed his lips to the side of her neck and his tongue formed circles on the sensitive skin.

Beatrice gasped when he cupped first one breast and then the other. With the pads of his fingers, he teased each tip until they were hard. Then to her delight, he took one into his mouth, while continuing to tease the other.

The longer he touched and kissed, the hotter her sex became, until she was rubbing her thighs together in an effort to relieve it.

"I think… ye should…join with me now," Beatrice gasped out each word.

This time when Duncan came over her, he seemed more assured, taking himself in hand and guiding himself to her entrance.

Beatrice cried out at the wonderful sensations their joining brought. Each one of his movements bringing more and more pleasure until she was sure to faint. On and on Duncan continued, seeming to gain momentum with each thrust, until slapping noises filled the room.

Unable to keep from it, Beatrice let go and allowed what would happen freedom and it was then the sensations of floating and then falling were joined by hot trails up and down her body.

She cried out when everything erupted at once, a feeling like none she'd ever encountered.

Unlike her, Duncan continued to seek his release. His large body was now drenched in sweat as he drove into her again and again. Hoarse grunts of pleasure echoed in her ears as he lost control, his movements jerky until with one last thrust, he spilled and cried out.

This time when he collapsed over her, Beatrice smiled into the darkness, sleep taking her away as she felt the bed move when Duncan slid off and left.

CHAPTER TEN

Despite waking alone in bed, Beatrice was in good spirits. Even the slight stiffness to her legs and back did not lessen her mood. There was much to do and if she was to establish herself as the lady of the estate, it was best to learn the house and see what all required her attention.

However, the first thing she needed was a bath. Moments after pulling the chord to a bell that sounded in the servant's common space, Orla appeared looking well rested.

The woman carried a tray with tea and toasted bread. "Good morning Lady Beatrice. Would ye like a bath to be drawn?"

"Aye, please," Beatrice replied hating the warmth of her cheeks. "Has Mister Duncan come downstairs yet?"

"He ate and left early this morning. Gara said he had something to take care of."

Curious that he'd gone. They'd just spoken the day before about remaining close for a fortnight.

By the time she bathed and ate it was late morning, and Beatrice felt as if she'd lost precious hours. She hurried into the kitchen to find Gara, but instead only Firtha was there.

"Good morning milady, what can I do for ye?" the woman asked with a bob.

"I wish to speak to Gara and learn about the duties of the

household," Beatrice said going to the window. "Is she outside?"

Firtha frowned. "No milady, she has gone to the market to make purchases to stock the larder and our pen outside."

"Why is the larder not already stocked?" Beatrice asked going to where Firtha motioned. "It seems odd to me, ye have had two people living here."

The woman nodded quickly. "Aye, we did at first. Keep it fully stocked, I mean. But most of it would go to waste. Mister Caelan eats last meal somewhere else most days and Mister Duncan usually eats only porridge in the morning here in the kitchen and then one meal in the late afternoon."

It made sense, a man living alone rarely had a need for a rigid schedule only to eat alone. Beatrice sighed. "I suppose we will have to discuss what our mealtimes will be now."

"I can show ye the house," Firtha said, glancing from her to Orla. "It is not as grand as Keep Ross, but there are enough rooms to be confusing at first."

Despite having walked through the house with Duncan, Beatrice was eager to see it all gain. "Very well."

They walked out of the kitchen and went to the left heading down a hallway that led to the main great room. From there, they went to the right to the servant's hallway. There were four bedchambers and each of the women who worked there had one. The rooms were small but much larger than what most servants could aspire to. Each had quality furniture and Beatrice liked that they also all had a window that looked out onto a wide-open field.

They returned to the great room and headed across to a short corridor that led to a parlor, a study that according to

Firtha only Caelan used.

Directly across a large beautifully decorated bedchamber. The furniture, much like the one in Duncan's bedroom had a four-poster bed and everything a person could need. Despite it, it was obvious not to be currently in use.

"Whose room was this?" Beatrice asked.

"Laird Ross. For when he visits."

"Ah, how delightful," Beatrice replied smiling. "My sister and her husband have their own space when they visit."

When they returned to the opening of the short hallway and went up the stairs. Beatrice and Duncan's bedchambers were on the left and on the right was a sitting room that Firtha informed them, Lady Mariel had planned to decorate.

Just past the sitting room was another bedroom, which Firtha explained was used by guests.

"Where does Mister Caelan sleep?" Beatrice asked.

They turned the corner and there was a set of doors, the last rooms on the second floor. "There," Firtha said pointing to the doors. "He uses two rooms, one to sleep and the other when he has company."

It seemed interesting to Beatrice that Caelan would take a room so far from the stairs, especially when only he and Duncan lived there.

Once the tour was done, to Beatrice it was evident that they required at least one more chambermaid and someone to ensure every other task was seen to. If she and Duncan were to have children, they'd also need a nursemaid.

"Are there any other bedchambers?" Beatrice asked. "I did not notice more than the four where ye, Gara, and Orla sleep."

"There is one more," Firtha replied. "Just past mine. It is a wee bit smaller, but very nice."

Good, it would be suitable for additional help.

For now, she'd have to wait on Gara to return and speak to her about it.

"Orla and I will go for a short walk to get familiar with the land. We will not go far."

Firtha frowned. "Mister Duncan said to ensure ye remained indoors. He is going to request that several guards from the keep be assigned here, to ensure ye are safe."

"Goodness," Beatrice said. "What about the grounds closest to the house? Surely, it will be safe to explore those."

Firtha led them to the doorway, and they continued outside. Next to the house was a small building that consisted of three large rooms. They peered into the first which was for washing laundry. The next two were a storeroom. The last was the largest space that had a table, chairs, and four beds where coachmen and guards that visitors brought with them slept.

"I suppose this is where our guards will live," Beatrice said looking around the room. "We must ensure the bedding is shaken out and that the room is swept."

Firtha nodded. "I will take care of it."

"I will help ye," Orla said, and they hurried off to find the needed supplies. In the meantime, Beatrice opened the windows to allow air in and peered out at the corral and stables.

There were two horses grazing and a man leaning on the fence looking off in the distance.

Firtha returned with Orla carrying brooms, rags, and buckets, Beatrice motioned out the window. "Firtha, where does he live?"

"Creagh MacDougal, takes care of the horses and lives out there in a room inside the stable. No family, just a hound. There." Firtha pointed to a dark dog that ran up to the man from the direction of the stables. Creagh, leaned over and patted the dog's head and then began walking around the corral, the dog on his heels.

"Would ye like some tea milady?" Firtha asked as she yanked bedding from the first bed and headed out the door.

"Nay. I do not require anything at the moment," Beatrice replied. "Please return to yer duties. I will assist Orla."

After a dubious look, Firtha left to see to the midday meal.

Beatrice followed Orla carrying two blankets. They went to a short fence, threw the blankets over it, and began to beat them with brooms. Once that was completed, they shook them.

"Just sweeping and dusting to do, I can finish up myself," Orla said.

"Very well. I will see about unpacking. Ye continue here," Beatrice replied.

The house seemed ominous in its silence when she walked back inside. It seemed so strange to her to be in an empty house. The entire time growing up, there were always people about at her home. At Keep Ross, the same. Family, servants, guards, and visitors came and went throughout the day.

Perhaps, once the chambermaid was hired and the new guards arrived, it would be a bit better. For now, it was as if she were the only person in the world.

She made her way up the stairs and walked past her bed-chamber and entered Duncan's. The bed was unmade, a tunic and breeches thrown across it.

Lying on the table was a cup, a comb, and a clan crest pin. His ceremonial tartan was folded and placed neatly next to the items.

Turning in a full circle, she couldn't help but feel that although he slept there, the room did not seem to belong to anyone. Then again, could it be her husband was like the space. Silent. Without adornment and half-empty.

When she tugged at the adjoining door, it didn't budge. The second time she pulled with both hands and it barely moved. Refusing to give in Beatrice took a deep breath, wrapped her hands around the long door handle, planted her feet, and yanked with all her might.

The door opened just enough for her to slip through.

As soon as she entered her own bedchamber, the ambiance was completely different. The air was perfumed from her favorite bath oils. The bed was made, her robe carefully draped over one of the front corners.

Hopefully, Gara would return before Duncan or else there would not be a presentable meal prepared. Beatrice supposed if need be, Firtha could cook something.

How had Duncan managed with only two people on his staff? It was unfathomable to her that he did not staff the house fully.

Thinking of his return, Beatrice hurried to the mirror to inspect her appearance. She hoped they would spend the evening together after eating last meal. With an uncompromising eye, she noted that her hair needed tending to. Despite helping with the bedding, her attire was more of someone planning to entertain and not for a wife home for the day.

After brushing her hair back in place, once again she

peered at her reflection. She decided not to change. The low neckline of her vest showcased the top of her breasts and she hoped the view would entice Duncan into her bed.

Lifting the delicate looking glass, she smiled at her reflection and then opened the envelope that had been placed next to it.

It was a sweet note from Isobel, wishing her happiness. Her lips curved and she folded it neatly and slipped it back into the envelope. It would be a keepsake.

With little else to do, she began to pull items from her trunk that she wished to have out. Some of her clothes were already put away and Orla would see about hanging up the rest of her dresses. That left only for her to find a place for each of her smaller personal belongings.

She set her notebooks on a table next to a chair, then her set of quill and ink next to them. After Beatrice took out her current needlepoint and set it into a basket that she'd found by the hearth, she placed it on the floor by the chair as well.

Once that was done, she pulled a dark shawl out of a trunk and draped it over the same chair. Then, she took in the room. It needed fresh items, either fruit or flowers. She went to the window and peered out.

A large lavender field grabbed her attention.

"Oh," Beatrice exclaimed, her lips curving. "Lavender," she said in an awestruck tone. Then she inhaled deeply drawing the perfumed air into her lungs.

The sound of voices reached her, and Beatrice walked out of the room. Since it was probably Firtha and Orla, she took her time walking down the stairs.

Instead, when she reached the bottom step, Duncan stood

in the entryway speaking to a man. The man's dark gaze flashed to Beatrice, but then returned to Duncan.

"Aye, I understand fully," the man said to Duncan and hurried back outside.

Duncan turned to her, his gaze sweeping over her sending tingles of awareness through her.

"Wife," he said by way of greeting. "Are ye alone?" He looked around the room. "Where is everyone?"

"Orla and Firtha are about. Gara went to the village."

He huffed. "I brought back four guardsmen. That one," he motioned to the door with his head, "is to be the lead guard. They are to sleep in the room next to the storeroom."

"Orla is cleaning the space now. However, I am not aware if Gara has returned as yet."

"There is time," Duncan replied. "The men must settle, and they will be content with a simple meal. Greer sent plenty of things for them to keep in their room."

The entire time he spoke to her, his gaze kept moving to her bosom, but he did not move closer. Instead, he seemed discomfited.

Beatrice wanted to laugh. She took his hand and pulled him toward the study. "I wish to ask ye something about this room," she purred.

His eyes narrowed. "The study?"

"Aye, it is quite dark do ye not think?"

When she pushed the door closed, the room became like a cave at night. She could just make out Duncan looking around the room. "It is Caelan's problem, not mine."

First one step, then another two, Beatrice moved closer. "It is a good private space to keep us from being seen, is it not?"

"Beatrice…"

"Kiss me, husband." Beatrice lifted to her tiptoes and turned her face up to him. Immediately his mouth covered hers and Duncan pulled her close. His kisses were new to her, the feel of his mouth enticing, and the taste of him intoxicating.

Beatrice clung to him, not wishing to ever separate. When his mouth traveled down the side of her neck to her cleavage and he lifted her breast from its bindings, she gasped.

The warmth of his mouth over first the left and then the right nipple made her knees weak. Thankfully, he held her up and continued to devour the offerings.

With her in his arms, he turned and lifted her onto Caelan's desk and pushed her skirts and shift up until fully exposing her. Then he fumbled with his own clothing, freeing himself.

"I have thought of nothing else but having ye again." The huskiness of his voice against Beatrice's ear made rivulets of heat travel up her body to between her legs.

Despite the desperate need to join, when Duncan prodded Beatrice's first reaction was to tense. Letting out several breaths, she pulled him closer. Needing the distraction of his mouth, she kissed him. Duncan's kisses had a powerful effect. His tongue pushed past her parted lips at the same time as he drove into her willing body.

Each movement was divine and the sounds he made like music to his ears. Beatrice cried out with each deep thrust. He stretched and filled her perfectly, their bodies seeming to be made for each other.

He continued driving in and out of her harder and faster,

and soon Beatrice could barely hold on to him. Whatever was on the desk crashed to the floor, the sounds adding to the excitement of the moment.

Beatrice cried out at the sensation of shattering and she dug her fingernails into the rough fabric of Duncan's tunic in an effort to keep from floating away.

When his hoarse moans filled her ears, she raked her fingers through his hair, taking his mouth once again greedily.

Duncan lifted her up and still joined managed to lower to the floor where he lay over Beatrice as he attempted to gain control of his breathing.

"This is wonderful. I am so happy to have married ye," Beatrice whispered.

He pressed a kiss to her temple. "Do not think this will keep me from yer bed tonight."

"Good," Beatrice replied with a giggle.

They finally stood and did what they could to arrange their clothing. Beatrice knew it was useless to return her hair to the same style, so she unbraided it and ran her fingers through it.

When they walked out of the study, the house remained eerily silent.

Orla appeared from the direction of the kitchen. "There ye are," she said with a bright smile.

By the sly look Orla slid to Duncan, the maid was perfectly aware of where they'd been and what they'd been doing. "Would ye like me to assist ye in dressing for last meal?"

Beatrice looked up to Duncan. "Do ye dress for last meal here?"

He shook his head. "It is yer home, ye can change things to how ye see fit."

"I will not change," Beatrice told Orla. "I would like tea and perhaps some toasted bread for my husband and I brought to the parlor, please."

Duncan followed her to the parlor. "Usually, a wife only brings a husband to the parlor when they have something to discuss."

"I do wish to discuss something with ye," Beatrice replied.

They sat in front of windows and she looked out to the lavender field. "I wish to speak to ye about yer expectations. Today, I wished to go for a walk and Firtha explained ye did not wish me to leave the house."

Her husband nodded. "There could be people about that are not trustworthy."

"Understandable. However, I would have liked it if ye would have told me directly and not informed me through someone on our staff."

"There are only Firtha and Gara…"

"And they are exhausted. The two of them cannot possibly maintain a house of this size now that I am here. I must insist on at least one more servant and a lad to help with menial tasks."

"Such as?"

"The cleaning of the hearths. Sweeping of the great room. Fetching water for the kitchen and for washing."

Beatrice continued, "Not only have Gara and Firtha done all of that, but they've also handled the cooking, gardening, and keeping the house clean. It is unfathomable that ye have not seen to more help."

"Very well. Ye can hire a woman and a lad. No more. I cannot have too many people about. I need privacy."

Beatrice was glad Lady Mariel had informed her of Duncan's horrid past, so she did not have to question him. "I understand. What is off-limits?"

"I bathe alone. No need to order baths for me." He thought for a long moment. "The area by the stone wall. No one is to go there or touch it. The guardsmen have already been told."

"I am sure Gara and Firtha will ensure to inform whoever comes to work here what is allowed."

After a discreet knock, Orla walked in with a tray. She set the items down and immediately left without a word.

Beatrice poured the tea and smiled up at Duncan. "I did not ask. Do ye drink tea?"

His lips lifted just a bit. "Aye, I do."

THE ENTIRE TIME Duncan and Beatrice enjoyed their simple repast, they exchanged heated looks. No sooner had she taken her last bite, did he push away from the table, round it, lift her into his arms, and race up the stairs.

CHAPTER ELEVEN

Duncan rolled over and yawned. Despite the drapes keeping his bedchamber dark, instinctively he knew it was morning. Very early morning.

Rubbing his eyes, he slid from the bed and pulled the long dark drapery apart to allow the dawn light in. There was little to do that day—like most days—he never planned for activities, other than working on the wall.

Just a short distance away, his project sat waiting for him. Creagh's continuously gleeful dog trotted to it and began sniffing. Then without a care in the world, lifted its leg and peed on the rocks he'd stacked.

Duncan shook his head. It was interesting that what was important to one being, meant absolutely nothing to another. The dog barked and raced after something, probably a rabbit. Duncan followed the dog's path until it stopped in its tracks and began barking, this time not friendly in the least.

Throwing open the window, he leaned out to ensure there wasn't a deadly threat to his stableman's pet.

A man at the edge of the woods appeared and brought his horse to a stop. The man sat very still, seeming to take in the house and its surroundings. It happened ever so often; a wayward traveler passing through, but something about this man brought an uneasy feeling.

The man didn't seem lost, not by the stillness and the way he continued to watch the house. Duncan considered different reasons for the rider's appearance. Someone seeking work, or perhaps one of Caelan's friends.

His brother never had visitors without first ensuring to notify him, and with his recent marriage, Caelan was staying at his mother's home for a short while to give them time alone.

The rider urged his mount closer, but upon the dog's barks becoming more menacing, he stopped and once again studied the house, his head moving to one side and then the other.

Although too far for Duncan to see the rider's features clearly, the rider seemed familiar. Instantly, he considered the fact that someone from his past would come for him. Not that they could take him away, but they would bring a reminder of things best left behind.

He whirled around, looking for his breeches, but then stopped at the sounds of hooves.

A second rider appeared, this one familiar. Creagh rode past his dog toward the man. His stableman called out a warning and asked who the man was and what he was doing there.

Silently the stranger held a hand up as if in greeting, turned his horse around, and galloped away.

The door between his and Beatrice's creaked. There was a loud feminine grunt and then it opened just enough for the beauty to slip through. Her wide eyes met his. "Did ye see what happened outside?"

She came to stand next to him and peered out the window. Creagh had dismounted and was down on one knee praising his dog.

"Aye, I am going to gather a pair of guardsmen and go after the man. He may not pose a threat, but I would rather be sure."

He frowned. "Where are the guardsmen that no one appeared at the stranger riding up so close to the house?"

After peering out the window for a moment longer, Beatrice shrugged. "I would venture to guess Gara and Firtha are holding court. They were very excited about having more mouths to feed and people filling the great room."

"I will have to inform both them and the guards they are not here as guests, but to work." He grunted his annoyance at the situation.

"I am sure once the assignments are made, the guardsmen will be responsible enough not to allow such things. Although, I do look forward to seeing their expressions when ye tell them yer stableman and his dog had to defend the house, while they were at a tea party."

Duncan pulled on his breeches and belted his tunic, while an already dressed Beatrice watched. It was strange that she did not comment on his scarred legs. Admittedly, only from just above the knee down was all that was bare.

The worse scars were on his back, the result of many whippings. That was something he wasn't sure he would ever be able to allow her to see.

"Come, let us see what happens."

They walked to the end of the hall and silently down the stairs. The great room was empty, but the sounds of conversation guided them to the kitchen.

The four guards sat around a table, empty plates in front of them. They were so engrossed in a story Gara told, that no one noticed him or Beatrice at the doorway. Firtha came up behind them and Duncan held a finger up to his lips for her to be silent.

Finally, a guard caught sight of them and immediately jumped to his feet. The others followed suit, while Gara looked perturbed at her story being interrupted.

"Men," Duncan said walking into the room. "Just outside a stranger on horseback appeared. But ye need not worry. The stableman and his dog ensured to keep ye safe."

The men shuffled uncomfortably, the younger one's face turning bright red.

Duncan pointed at one and then another. "Both of ye, go out and look for any sign of him. Ask Creagh for a description."

Looking to the other two, he continued, "Ye two guard the house until morning, then we will switch." He looked to the first man who'd gotten to his feet. "I leave ye to manage the assignment of tasks."

The guards hurried out.

"It was my fault to have kept them here." Gara sniffed and wiped at her eyes with the edge of her apron.

"Do not fash yerself," Duncan told her in a warm tone. "Just remember they are here to work and not as company."

"Aye," Gara said and Firtha went to her and patted her shoulders. The younger woman gave them an apologetic look. "I will bring yer meal immediately."

"Come let us sit," Beatrice slipped her arm around Duncan's right one and they walked to the adjacent dining room.

Once seated, she let out a sigh. "I wish to speak to ye about something." Her blue gaze met his. "Will ye consider staying in my bedchamber tonight?"

"Is something wrong?" Perhaps the appearance of the stranger had scared his wife. He wasn't used to a woman's sensibilities and could not fathom why she'd want him in her bed all night.

Admittedly, he'd woken several times hard as a rock and had considered going back to her bed. However, he'd forced himself to remain in his bedchamber, unsure she would welcome such an intrusion.

"Nothing is wrong really," she admitted, but then sighed. "I am lonely. I miss my sister and family. I know it's silly, but the last two nights I wake from sleep and cry. I feel so very alone."

Thankfully Firtha hurried in with their food, giving him additional time to come up with a good reply. He was not sure about spending the night in her bedchamber. The temptation would be too great after making love to remain without clothing. It would leave too many opportunities for bad things to happen.

What if he had a nightmare and hurt her? Or if she caught a glimpse of his back and refused him in her bed again?

Beatrice watched him, which led Firtha to do the same and Duncan realized he had remained silent and frozen in place.

"Is something wrong Mister Duncan?" Firtha asked, her worried gaze moving from him to Beatrice, who also studied him with concern.

"No, nothing." He waved the woman away. "Thank ye."

"So, the answer is no," Beatrice said, anger transforming her face. Lips in a tight line and brows furrowed, she looked like an adorable angry kitten. "Fine."

He struggled with an explanation. "Ye do not understand. I am not accustomed to sharing a bed."

"Neither am I husband," she replied emphasizing the word "husband".

"I may roll over and hurt ye. I am much larger and heavier than ye…" he began.

She huffed. "It is a wonder Isobel is still alive then?" It was true, Darach was much larger than her sister.

"They share a bedchamber?"

Beatrice gave him a droll look. "Since the day they married."

The back of his neck came to life, itching and he scratched it. "I am not sure what to say. I will consider it. The time I was in captivity has affected me in ways that ye cannot understand. I do not wish to hurt ye if I wake from a dream and am blinded by it."

"Then I would wake ye with a sharp slap. Which, I am so very tempted to do at the moment." Beatrice pushed from the table and rushed from the room.

Orla walked in with a tea kettle. "I was to refresh her tea…" She looked to Beatrice's untouched plate. "Is she unwell?"

"No just angry," Duncan replied getting up and walking out past Orla. "Tell her I've gone to the village to find my brother."

The fact his wife was angry with him did not feel good. When walking past the stairwell, his chest tightened. For a moment he considered going to her, but decided he would only make her angrier when he did not change his mind about her request.

Once outside in the fresh morning air, it felt so good that instead of going to the stable to fetch his horse, he went to the wall. Stacking a few stones would help him think clearer. If nothing else, the activity would ease the tension in his shoulders.

The first stone was so heavy, his entire body shook as he lifted it up to rest on the top of his thighs. Duncan blew out breaths then heaved it up to the wall. It was much too heavy, and it proved impossible. He jumped back as the stone crashed to the ground.

"Blast it all," he exclaimed then bent over to catch his breath.

"A two-man job, that one," Creagh said nearing. The dog galloped towards them, its tongue hanging from its mouth.

"Did ye get a clear view of the horseman?"

"A bit," Creagh said, his booted foot pushing at the large stone. "No one familiar to me."

"Hope the guards catch up to him," Duncan said and eyed the stone. "I need a few moments before trying again."

He studied the quiet man. "Why are ye not married?"

"I was once, but my wife died. Never could find another like her."

Duncan looked toward the house. "Mine is angry with me right now."

Creagh's deep chuckles seemed to bounce off the wall. "Aye, that is a common occurrence when passion is present. Treasure these moments."

"Why would I treasure her being cross?" Duncan said preparing mentally to attempt to lift the large stone again.

"Ye will know when she gives ye a reprieve," Creagh replied. The man waited for Duncan to lift the stone and once again rest it on his upper thighs. When he took a deep breath to lift it to the wall, Creagh only assisted when it teetered on the edge. Together, they pushed with care to ensure it didn't tumble over the opposite side.

Duncan climbed on top of the wall and shimmied the stone into place. Despite being winded, each time a new stone was placed, satisfaction of accomplishment filled him.

Creagh's dog barked and jumped up and down thinking him being atop the wall was a great game. Duncan jumped down and the happy dog ran in circles around him.

"Stop!" Creagh ordered, but the dog ignored him. "Go!" He ordered, this time the dog stopped and looked to see what direction Creagh pointed in. The dog took off in the direction of Creagh's arm.

"Where is he going?" Duncan asked as the dog raced toward the stables.

"Probably to annoy the horses." Creagh chuckled. "Donan is a good companion to me. I know he can be irritating."

"I like him," Duncan said. "He is a good dog."

When Creagh walked away, Duncan remained at the wall. He lifted a smaller stone and placed it on the wall and once again climbed atop to make adjustments. Straightening, he could see far into the distance. There was no one in sight, not even on the road that traveled alongside the edge of his land.

It was a quiet day and he wondered what Beatrice was doing at the moment. If he was a normal man, he'd go inside and ensure her happiness. Perhaps with a tumble in bed. But he was not normal and despite their being together without clothing, he'd not allowed any light in the room.

Her feeling his scarred chest against her delicate, creamy skin was nothing compared to seeing it in bright daylight.

Their interlude in Caelan's study had been quite enjoyable, but he doubted she would wish for something like that at the moment.

It was best that he go in search of his brother and find out if a friend came to visit. If the stranger was nothing more than a wayward traveler, then he would not worry about it. But for some reason, something about the man had given him pause.

After having to survive on his instincts for so many years, Duncan had learned to trust his gut reaction.

He went to the stables and saddled a horse. Upon mounting, he guided the animal to where Creagh was. "If my brother happens to come home, inform him I must speak with him and to remain. I am riding to his mother's home."

The day was sunny, the aroma of fresh lavender from the nearby field mixed perfectly with the scent of salty sea air. He inhaled deeply filling his lungs and looked up to the sky. Never would he take the feeling of freedom for granted. Some days the open surroundings overwhelmed Duncan. There was nothing like the choice to go as far as one wished. Not being bound to a pole, to see the sky, and to breathe fresh air was a privilege.

Caelan's mother's home was near a large village and when he arrived, a worker informed him that his half-brother had gone to the tavern.

Turning in the direction of the village, Duncan searched the area for the man who he'd seen that morning, but he was not among the few people he encountered along the road.

The men in the tavern turned to the doorway and watched

Duncan with curiosity, only a few acknowledging him. He rarely went to the village and it was even rarer that he'd make an appearance at the only tavern.

"Oy, brother," Caelan called from a corner table where he sat with another man. Duncan recognized him as one of the landholders that lived in the land next to theirs.

The man went to stand, but Duncan held up his right hand. "Please stay, I wish to inform ye about something."

Both men looked up at him with curiosity. As Duncan explained about the horseman who'd appeared out of the woods, both Caelan and the other man exchanged looks of concern.

"One of my men told me about a man appearing after the night of the storm. Matches yer description. I assumed he was a traveler who may have taken shelter in my woods during the storm."

Caelan frowned. "Perhaps, he is searching for work."

"I thought the same," Duncan replied and looked to their companion. "He did not come to ask for work, did he to ye?"

"Nay," the man replied.

Duncan proceeded to tell them about sending guardsmen out to search. The others agreed it was best to find out who the man was.

"I will ask my workers if anyone has spotted him again and send word if I learn something useful," the man said before taking his leave.

"A drink?" A busty woman came to the table leaning so far over that her breasts were on the brink of spilling from her bodice. Both he and Caelan stared at the offered view.

"Ale," Duncan said dragging his gaze from the woman's

bosoms that suddenly brought the thought of having Beatrice's in his mouth.

"Same," Caelan said not bothering to look away.

When the wench returned with the drinks, she went to Caelan's side of the table and he took full advantage pressing his lips to the top of her right breast.

The woman giggled with delight, and soon Caelan's face was buried between them.

The woman gave Duncan a wanton look inviting him to join. For the first time in his life, he considered it, feeling experienced since he'd made love several times now. The woman was attractive, with green eyes and auburn curls. She was voluptuous and would make for good bedsport. However, he would not betray his vows. Just considering her invitation, he felt as if he'd been unfaithful, and it wasn't a good feeling.

"I promise more later, Sariah," Caelan said pushing her away gently. "Right now, I must speak with my brother." The woman allowed Caelan to kiss her and then after a wink to Duncan walked away.

"Ye have laid with her before?" Duncan asked.

Caelan nodded. "Aye and so have others. For a price." His brother turned his attention to Duncan. "What is this about guardsmen? Why did ye not inform me?"

"I am informing ye now. It is necessary, especially after realizing that sometimes wanderers are about." Duncan took a swig of his ale. "Ye should also know that Beatrice wishes to hire a chambermaid and a lad to help with menial chores."

"Do ye think it is absolutely necessary?" Caelan's brows fell. "Ye are used to very few people being about."

A part of him wondered the same. However, now that he

was married, it was to be Beatrice's home as well and he didn't wish for her to want for anything.

"I married a laird's daughter. I expect that she prefers to have help with things. I didn't tell her that ye and I are who clean out the hearths and chop wood for cooking and for the fireplaces."

Caelan chuckled. "I am going to miss my only form of exercise."

"If she only hires a lad, then we can still chop wood. I do not plan to stop. The lad can take the wood inside and to the different rooms."

"Different rooms?" Caelan asked. "Where do ye mean?"

"The great room, yer study, our bedchambers."

"It is the same number of rooms as before, Gara and Firtha have always carried their own from what we brought into the kitchen."

Duncan decided to gauge Caelan's reaction to Beatrice sleeping in a separate bedchamber.

"There is also Beatrice's room."

His brother did not seem affected at all by the announcement. "That is one additional room. I do not see why ye and I cannot carry our own and ye to an additional room."

"I will give her what she asks. It is not too much; however, I did advise against more servants or help."

"Good," Caelan said. "Inform her of yer mother's invasion once a season with her army of servants." They both drank deeply from their cups at the thought of the days they both hid away from his mother.

Duncan was enjoying time with Caelan. Since he'd moved into the house, they'd become close and there was little he did not share with his brother.

"I must ask," Caelan said looking around to ensure not to be overheard. "How have ye dealt with intimacy? Do ye have any questions?"

He'd expected Caelan's curiosity. Duncan told him of what Darach had instructed and of how it had gone so far. He left out the interlude in Caelan's study while wondering if Beatrice had ordered that the room be put back in order.

"Sounds like ye have things well in hand," Caelan affirmed. "I think ye should consider allowing her to see all of ye, little by little. Making love in other than darkness is very enjoyable."

"I cannot," Duncan said firmly.

"How about her family? What are yer plans?"

CHAPTER TWELVE

"WE SHOULD HAVE alerted the guards," Orla said as they walked to the nearby lavender field. "If one of us gets hurt and has to hobble back, Mister Duncan will be very angry that no one was about to help us."

Beatrice chuckled. "Ye wish for a strong man to carry ye back? Why did ye not tell me, I would have ensured the one of yer choice came with us and then pushed ye down so he would have to."

"Lady Beatrice!" Orla exclaimed, her cheeks growing bright pink. "I did not mean for that..."

"I jest with ye," Beatrice replied. "It is a romantic idea. Ye are not being courted are ye?"

Orla shook her head, her pert nose wrinkling. "Nay. I have never been pursued. I am not a beauty, so I suppose men do not take notice."

Taking her in, Beatrice first noticed Orla's mop of curls that tumbled past her shoulders. Her hair was lovely and thick, but unruly. She normally wore it in a bun at the nape of her neck, but by midday, half of the hair had escaped its confines. The clothes Orla wore were what was expected of a servant. However, the dresses were always faded and heavily mended. The edges of her skirts were frayed, as was the cap that currently sat lopsided atop her head.

"Why do ye have so few clothes and those ye have seem very old?"

Orla looked down at her stained apron. "I only came to work at Keep Ross recently. My last mistress died, and her son and his wife moved into the house.

The woman took an instant dislike to me and reduced my wages. I barely had enough for necessities. Once I saved up, with only half an afternoon off every fortnight, there was little time to purchase fabrics and even less to sew a dress."

"Yer a beauty Orla. Ye must get new clothing as soon as possible. We must make changes immediately."

As they walked and filled their baskets with lavender, they planned a trip to the village to purchase fabric. Beatrice planned to sew table coverings and drapes for Duncan's bedroom, to lighten up the space. "We must visit a seamstress and order serviceable dresses for us both. I only brought frivolous gowns for my visit to South Uist—not expecting to remain—therefore, I do not have anything that will serve me well day-to-day."

A man on horseback appeared. He dismounted and allowed the horse to graze. Beatrice and Orla exchanged looks.

"Is that the same man ye saw earlier?" Orla asked, her eyes wide.

Beatrice studied the man and horse. "It could be. He was too far. We should be cautious. Let us walk back."

"Lady Beatrice," the man called out. "Are ye not Duncan Ross's new bride?"

Beatrice narrowed her eyes at the man. "How do ye know my name?"

The man neared. He was not unattractive and seemed to

be a bit older than Duncan. He had shoulder-length light brown hair and dark eyes. A scar from the outer corner of his left eye to the side of his mouth gave him a dangerous air. Yet his demeanor was not threatening.

"Yer husband and I spent many years together on a ship. There is little I do not know about him."

Beatrice looked over her shoulder. They had not gone so far. If she or Orla screamed, the guards would hear. "I will have to insist ye come and visit us then. Perhaps tomorrow? I am sure Duncan will be glad to see ye. What is yer name?"

"Farlan Reid," he replied and looked past her to the house. "I am not sure he will be as welcoming as ye. However, I will ask that ye convey my congratulations on the marriage. I wish ye well." The man bowed and turned away, returning to his horse.

Orla frowned. "Very interesting. Do ye think he will come to visit?"

"I do not know. I am sure Duncan will have an opinion."

They were met halfway back by an out of breath guardsman, who'd obviously raced to find them.

"Lady Beatrice. Ye must inform us…when…ye…"

Beatrice took pity on him and interrupted so he could catch his breath. "I do apologize. We did not plan to walk so far, but upon seeing the lavender we came to cut some for the house." When she looked over her shoulder, Farlan Reid was gone.

The guard motioned for them to walk ahead as he followed.

Meeting Orla's gaze, Beatrice shook her head. "Perhaps it will be best if I do not mention what just happened."

"I think ye are right," Orla said sneaking a look to the guard who followed them.

Upon returning home, Beatrice and Orla spent the day placing lavender into vases and tying some into bunches to be hung in the bedchambers and parlor.

When Gara announced last meal, Beatrice was annoyed that Duncan was still absent. She insisted Orla eat with her, so she didn't have to eat alone.

"We will go to the village tomorrow," Beatrice told Gara. "Please ask Creagh to prepare a coach and horses for first thing in the morning."

"Aye, milady," the woman replied. "I left word in the village that there was a need for help. Orla can see about it while ye are there."

A plan in place, Beatrice was excited for the next day. The only thing that dampened her spirits was her husband's absence.

WITH DUNCAN'S BEDCHAMBER empty, Beatrice could not relax. She'd already detained Orla until the poor woman yawned so wide her jaw cracked. Now she sat in the bed, her gaze fixed on the door between her and Duncan's room that she had left slightly ajar.

Every so often she went to the window and peered toward the stables hoping to catch a glimpse of his return.

Finally, footsteps sounded. He went into his bedchamber and she hurried to peek in. Duncan stood in front of his door visibly swaying. He stumbled to a chair and dropped into it. When he attempted to remove his boot and fell out of the chair, he chuckled.

Then putting a finger to his mouth made loud shushing noises. Her husband was drunk.

Caelan entered the room and stood over Duncan. "Ye are making too much noise."

"My boosh refushees to come off," Duncan slurred.

It seemed to Beatrice that Caelan was also in his cups, but not quite as much as Duncan. The brother managed to help Duncan back onto the chair and removed his boots. Then he helped him to the bed.

"Look," Caelan ordered and Duncan lifted his head.

"What?"

"I am pushing this bashin here. Ush it if ye get sick."

Duncan managed a nod. "I will."

Mere moments after Caelan walked out, Duncan's snores filled the air.

Beatrice slipped through the doorway and tiptoed to the bed. Fast asleep, Duncan lay face down, his head on the edge of the bed. Each exhalation was a loud snore.

Bending closer, she sniffed at his face. "Whisky," she whispered. There was another distinct smell, and it was not something he enbibed. It was a flowery scent, like that a woman wore.

"Where were ye?" Beatrice slapped his shoulder. "Who were ye with?"

The response was an incoherent mumble and another pair of snores. She would have to wait until morning to get an answer. If not from him, then his brother would answer for what they'd been doing until so late.

Annoyed, she paced and then decided it was best to try to get sleep. She had plans for the following day. Once she questioned Duncan, a trip to the village could not be delayed.

The prospect of another night alone in her bedchamber loomed and she let out a breath. Duncan was much too out of his wits to know if she slept there. No doubt he would not wake until late, which gave her the opportunity to get up and slip back to her own bedchamber.

Beatrice rounded the bed, slid between the blankets, and promptly fell into an exhausted slumber.

"Do not hit me. I will do whatever ye want."

Sobbing sounded.

"No, please, I will do whatever ye want. It hurts so much."

Beatrice woke with a start to find that she was still in Duncan's bed. It was still dark, and he was still asleep. At least she thought him to be.

He was curled into a ball, his arms around his head. "Not again. I cannot take more." He sounded weak, desperate, and helpless. His entire body shook as the dream seemed to take a horrible turn.

When he arched and screamed as if being struck, Beatrice slid from the bed and lowered down to her knees on the opposite side of where he slept.

"Please stop. I beg ye. I am begging. I will do what ye ask." This time his cries were quiet as he seemed to accept whatever fate his tormentor had asked of him.

Beatrice did not wish to imagine what he'd been forced to do all those years as a captive. What had been done to him, against his will. She covered her mouth with both hands to keep from crying out when he began to sob again.

When morning came, Beatrice was back in her own room. After dressing for the day, she went down the stairs. No one was about, so she went to the kitchen to pour herself something to drink. The aroma of cinnamon reminded her of home and early mornings in the kitchen with her mother.

By the time she drank her tea, Orla informed her that Caelan and Duncan were in the dining room. "They do not look well at all."

"Too much drink. I remember mornings after my brothers overindulged," Beatrice said with a grimace. "They would have the worst tempers."

She refilled her cup and made her way to where the men were. Duncan's gaze immediately met hers, he seemed to be gauging her mood. She made sure to keep her expression blank.

"How are ye husband? Caelan?" she asked sitting down. "Ye both do not look well."

Caelan replied, "I must take the blame for insisting Duncan celebrate yer marriage. We ended up drinking more than we should have."

"Is that true?" Beatrice asked turning to Duncan.

Her husband's eyes widened just a bit. "Aye, we did celebrate."

"Am I to assume more than one woman was involved in this …celebration?" She focused on a love bite on Caelan's neck. He rubbed the spot and immediately inspected Duncan's.

"Only one and she was with me," Caelan said.

Duncan's reddish eyes met hers. "I will never violate my vows to ye."

"Orla and I are going to the village," Beatrice informed her husband. "Creagh is taking us."

The men exchanged glances. "Should a guard accompany ye?" Caelan asked.

"How far is it?" Beatrice asked.

"An hour at most," Duncan replied. "I believe having Creagh along may be enough."

The rest of the meal was eaten mostly in silence. Caelan made an effort to ask her what plans she had for the house and staff. For the most part, he seemed in agreement and Beatrice was glad for it. Despite not knowing Duncan's half-brother well, she felt they could get along.

"I am going to do a bit of work," Caelan informed them and then looked to Beatrice. "I do the bookkeeping. If ye have any questions or would like to know anything about the finances, please come to my study and I will explain."

After he walked out of the room, Beatrice gave Duncan a pointed look. "Ye smelled of flowers last night."

"When did ye smell me?" he asked seeming genuinely perplexed.

"Must I remind ye that we have adjoining rooms? I over-heard ye arriving and checked to ensure ye were unharmed. That is when I smelled both the whiskey and the fragrance."

For a long moment he considered what to say. It was obvi-ous by the changing expressions that he discarded one idea after another.

"I do not remember clearly. However, I am prepared to get on one knee and promise that nothing occurred between a woman and myself."

She met his gaze. "I believe ye. I trust ye. Who I do not trust husband, are other women." Beatrice finished eating and pushed away from the table. "It is best I go, do not wish to miss the best offerings at the village square."

"Do ye require coin?"

Beatrice thought about it. She had money of her own but decided to save it just in case it was needed. "Aye, I do."

She followed Duncan up the stairs to his bedchamber. When they entered, he avoided looking at the rumpled bed and instead went to the trunk. He lifted the top just enough to slide his hand into it and brought out a small leather sack.

"Let me know if ye require more." He handed her the heavy sack.

"This is too much," Beatrice said barely able to hold the coin bag in her hand.

Duncan pressed a kiss to her cheek. "Ye must have enough to get whatever ye need for the house."

THE VILLAGE WAS much like villages near her home. It was smaller than the one closer to Keep Ross, but it was lively. The tavern anchored the square and several other familiar buildings completed it. There was a mill, a butcher, a blacksmith, and several others; all with their shingles ensuring visitors were aware of what was offered.

She and Orla asked where they might find a seamstress and then had to chase after an excited young lass, who raced up one street after the other until she came to a small house.

They entered a doorway to a large room filled with fabric and trimmings. A woman greeted them, her keen gazing moving over her dress.

After Beatrice informed her of what she wished to purchase for herself and Orla, the woman called for a younger version of herself to help with measurements. Beatrice enjoyed choosing from the assortment of fabrics, picking mostly browns, tans, and a few black items. For Orla, she chose a light-colored fabric for special days and then three service dresses in natural tones.

They stopped at the shoemaker's, and each found a pair of boots that fit. Afterwards, they purchased, yarn, thread, several blankets, a pair of baskets, and wooden bowls to be used on the table for both food and flowers.

While the carriage was loaded, Beatrice returned to the square and to the delight of the merchants purchased something from each stand.

Beatrice followed Ella's advice and introduced herself to the people as the new mistress of the Ross estate house. The villagers seemed to hold Duncan in high esteem and congratulated her while sending their regards to her husband.

Out of the corner of her eye, she caught a glimpse of the same man who'd been to her house and Beatrice hurried to him.

"Ye left without responding to my invitation," Beatrice said noting the man seemed discomfited by her sudden appearance.

Ensuring no one could see, he reached for her left wrist and pulled her closer. "Ye should forget to have ever seen me." His face hardened. "Tis best if yer husband has no knowledge that we spoke at yer home or here at the village. I will not be coming to yer house."

"Why would ye not wish him to see ye?"

The dark gaze locked with hers and his lips curled into a

toothy smile. "When I said I knew everything and shared much with yer husband, I meant it. He and I grew very close while at sea for so many years."

Beatrice attempted to snatch her hand away, but he did not release it. His face pressed against the side of hers and he whispered in her ear. "I fucked yer husband. Ask him about that."

Her mouth fell open at the unbelievable words the man uttered. "Ye are a horrible person," she exclaimed. "I will certainly not ask him that. Release me, sir!"

At her voice rising, he released her, but his lips remained in the evil grin. "Aye, ye are not the only one who knows Duncan Ross intimately."

Beatrice's heart thundered as Farlan Reid strolled away seeming happy to have shared what he did. The only reason she was aware of men laying together was because one of her cousins, Albert, preferred men to women and had once admitted it her.

It was whispered about during family gatherings when her cousin often attended with another man, who remained at his side. Despite the fact he preferred men, Albert was Beatrice's favorite cousin to spend time with. He was entertaining and very charismatic.

"What did he say?" Orla whispered frantically. "Ye are very pale."

Beatrice shook her head, unable to speak.

Could it be the real reason Duncan did not wish to marry? Did her husband prefer men? Beatrice returned to the carriage with Orla, both of their arms laden with purchases.

She sat back in the soft seat her mind awhirl. How would

she bring it up to Duncan? Lead in with the fact she was aware some men preferred those of their same sex?

Farlan was the horseman who'd been watching the house. It could be he was heartbroken over losing Duncan.

What a mess she found herself in, if that man was truly who Duncan wished to be with.

When she took a shaky breath, Orla gave her a worried look. "Ye seem about to cry. What is wrong?"

"I am so very tired. Some days I wish I were back home in North Uist and not be so impetuous to do things."

The entire ride to her home, Beatrice's mind was awhirl. Could she possibly speak to Duncan about Farlan's allegations? She feared his reaction more than anything. Even if what the man had said was true, Duncan could retaliate violently. But not with her, of that, she was sure.

She closed her eyes thinking perhaps it would be best to avoid him altogether. By the time they returned it would be close to last meal and she could claim a headache and go straight to bed.

With a plan in mind, she felt better.

Too soon they arrived at the house. Duncan emerged from the house to meet the carriage; his demeanor warm as he helped her climb out. Insisting on carrying her purchases, he waited for her to go inside and followed.

"Did ye enjoy the village?" he asked as they placed the bundles on a table in the great room.

She met his gaze hoping to sense something from him that she'd not seen before. Instead, she saw warmth and genuine interest.

"Orla and I ordered dresses from the seamstress. She is a

lovely woman and was so grateful. We also bought fabric and baskets." As she spoke, Beatrice pulled out several bundles and showed the items to Duncan. "Before leaving, I introduced myself to every merchant in the square and purchased something from each one as well. I did enjoy that very much."

"Oh, I almost forgot," Beatrice said lifting her foot. "I got new boots."

He inspected her foot. "The shoemaker does good work." He lifted a small bag and sniffed it. "What is this?"

"Herbs for teas and some for poultices and such. I purchased a few different ones and some jars to keep them in."

Duncan snatched her right arm and lifted it. "What happened to yer wrist?"

"Oh… I stumbled and got it caught in…" She couldn't think fast enough.

"The truth Beatrice." His gaze locked with hers. "Ye are not a good liar."

She let out a breath. "Promise me ye will not get angry and do something rash."

Duncan stared at her wrist. "I cannot promise."

"Then I will not tell ye."

For a few moments they locked gazes, until Caelan walked into the room. "Am I interrupting?"

Beatrice turned to Caelan. "Duncan wishes me to tell him what happened to my wrist, but he will not promise to not become angry."

The men exchanged looks. "Ye should tell him. Duncan is not a violent person, he will go for a walk and put stones upon his wall if angered."

She wasn't sure either of them was prepared for what she

had to say. "I am not sure if I should divulge what happened to both of ye, or just ye," Beatrice met Duncan's gaze. "Perhaps, I can tell Caelan, and he can find the best way to convey the information to ye."

"Just tell me," Duncan said. "There are no secrets between me and my brother."

"Hmmm," Beatrice thought about what Farlan had said.

"Very well," Beatrice said. "Let us go to the parlor."

They walked into the parlor, which seemed so much smaller with both men inside.

"Yesterday, while ye both were at the tavern, Orla and I went for a short walk. We picked the lavender." She motioned to the flowers in a vase. "A man appeared and congratulated me on our marriage. He claimed to know ye, Duncan. He asked me to convey his good wishes and I invited him to come to the house and see ye."

When neither spoke, she continued. "I saw him again at the village today. This time he tried to avoid me. I followed him and asked why he'd not responded to my invitation. He took me by the wrist and said I should forget ever seeing him and not to mention it to ye."

"What else?" Duncan said his voice seeming hollow, his gaze boring into her.

"He said ye and he were once very close." Beatrice leaned forward and looked at Caelan. "Very close."

Caelan coughed and pressed his lips together as if trying not to laugh. "Why did he hold yer wrist so hard?"

Beatrice shrugged. "It was as if he was desperate that I did not tell Duncan I had seen him." She returned her attention to her husband. "He said it was best ye did not know he was here."

"Did he give ye a name," Duncan said dryly. "I am sure it is someone angry over me beating him in the games. I will find whoever it is and ensure they do not spread lies about me again."

"How close did he say they were?" Caelan asked sliding a look to Duncan.

"I do not find the accusations one bit humorous," Duncan snapped.

Beatrice frowned. "He said ye and he had...been intimate." Both she and Caelan watched Duncan for a reaction, and she at least was surprised when he didn't react. Instead, he gave her a droll look. "What is the man's name, wife?"

"Farlan Reid," Beatrice replied dryly. "I have to admit to being shocked that a man would say such a thing publicly. Someone could be hanged just for speaking about participating in such a thing."

"Very true," Caelan said as he stood and came to Beatrice, blocking her view of Duncan. "Come with me, I wish to speak to ye about some changes ye may wish to make in the house."

Beatrice glanced around Caelan to Duncan, who looked at her and nodded. "Go on, I must speak to the guards about a man being able to approach ye without them knowing."

"A guard did come when he saw what happened. The man, Farlan, left before the guard arrived. I informed the guard he was an acquaintance. So do not punish them for it."

Once she and Caelan went to the dining room, Beatrice spoke in a low tone. "Are ye sure he will not do anything rash?"

"If my brother wishes to beat the man to a pulp for bruising yer wrist, I will not blame him," Caelan replied in a curt tone. "I would do the same. Do not hold him back from it."

CHAPTER THIRTEEN

THE GATHERING OF clouds and grey skies promised rain and colder weather to come. Duncan guided his horse through the woods keeping his gaze forward, not bothering to worry about a possible attack.

He knew exactly where to find Farlan. Not because there were only a few places to hide, but because he knew and understood him. The man had spoken the truth in that they'd grown to know each other well. However, they'd never been intimate. He was sure Farlan had said that to Beatrice to draw him out.

"I want to die," Farlan said, gasping out each word. The man shook with the aftereffects of the harsh blows he'd just received. His left arm was misshapen and swelling.

Stretching as far as his chain allowed, Duncan was able to grab a rag from a pile they used to dress with or cleaning tasks. He tore one to strips, tied it together to make it longer, and then crawled to where Farlan lay. The feverish man, used to pain, barely made a sound as he set the arm and wrapped the makeshift bandages around it. Unfortunately, their tormentors would probably use the broken arm as a weapon against Farlan, to make him do whatever they asked.

Some days either he or Farlan would resist doing whatever

horrible tasks they were forced to do. It mattered little because the beatings were a source of entertainment for their captors and often whether they acquiesced or not, there would be punishment.

"What did they want ye to do this time?" Duncan asked looking up at the ceiling. If Farlan had not done what they wanted, then it was possible they would want him to.

"Fight against the big one... or be thrown overboard." Farlan's voice was low and faraway. "I ran toward the side, hoping to jump, but they stopped me and hung me by my arm until I lost consciousness."

From the bruising on Farlan's face, Duncan realized he'd had to fight with one broken arm.

He went back to his side of the dirty room and lay on his side. It was best not to be found caring for Farlan. For some reason it angered their captors.

They were on a Spanish ship. Had been traded to them just months earlier after a battle. A peace offering of sorts.

Their captors hated the British and although both Duncan and Farlan were Scots, the Spanish didn't seem to realize it, or care.

"Help me die," Farlan said lifting his head to look at Duncan. "I beg ye. Kill me."

There was a path made by the wildlife and Duncan guided his horse down it until he reached a clearing. There he dismounted and walked around the clearing looking through the trees for movement.

It wasn't long before Farlan appeared. Immediately Duncan was transported back to the years that he fought daily to forget. "Why did ye approach my wife?"

Despite being only about five years older than him, Farlan had aged a great deal. His hair graying. His face drawn and scarred.

He had a slight limp and his left arm remained bent at an odd angle. The dark eyes that met his were filled with hate. "Is that what ye really want to ask me?"

"There is nothing else for us to speak about."

Farlan's lips twisted into a misshapen smile. "Ye left me to die."

"Do ye really think I was in any shape to do more than survive? I was thrown overboard, half-crazed with whatever illness I had contracted. It was by pure happenstance that I was found and rescued."

"We swore to return for the other," Farlan yelled. "Ye did not keep yer word to me."

"What do ye want from me?" Duncan asked holding his arms out. "That we are both free is a miracle."

Farlan huffed and held out his right arm in the direction of Duncan's home. "Ye have a grand home, a beautiful wife, servants..." He hesitated as if searching for words. "I lost everything. The year before I was finally released, the last of my family perished. I was not there to stop it."

"That is not my fault," Duncan said. "The blame for all our misfortunes lies on the heads of our captors."

"They are dead," Farlan said with an unfocused look past him. "I hunted every single one of them down and ensured they suffered. They all died begging me to kill them."

It was then Duncan understood he was on the man's list of people he planned to kill. He took the man in. Although smaller than him and not fit, Farlan was used to fighting past pain and would also be strengthened by hatred and the need for revenge.

"Ye should give yerself the opportunity to enjoy life. After what we went through, we deserve to have good things happen." Duncan's sword was strapped to his back, Farlan had no visible weapon.

"I am living and doing exactly what I wish," Farlan replied walking closer. "Do ye not see that this is what gives me a reason to rise in the mornings?"

At one point Duncan had also plotted revenge. However, over the years the urge had become weaker. "How long has it been since ye escaped?"

A bark of laughter erupted from deep in Farlan's chest. "Escape." He laughed bitterly. "I was starved until barely conscious and then like ye, thrown overboard to die. Eight years ago."

Farlan shook his head. "Despite being held with ye all those years, ye never told me where ye came from. I had to search for a long time."

He'd purposely never spoken of home; it was too painful. Obviously, it had bought him years of reprieve from Farlan's quest to kill him.

When Farlan moved closer, Duncan considered unsheathing his sword. "I do not wish to fight ye. Return to yer home and start over."

"Do not dare tell me how to live my life. Do ye not see? I have nothing to live for." Farlan motioned to his midsection. "I can never lie with a woman; my manhood was damaged. Ye remember that do ye not? Or is it something ye also chose to forget?"

"I remember it all, ye included. We were captives, chained in the same place for years. How can I not remember?"

"Ye left me to die," Farlan insisted.

"I am not responsible for ye. I wanted to help. I tried to find the ship, but it was gone by the time I recovered."

The disbelief in Farlan's face made Duncan stop attempting to explain. The man was mad with hatred and would not hear or allow anything to distract him from what he planned.

"Kneel before me," Farlan said, his gaze locking with Duncan's. "Beg for yer life."

The words were familiar. It was what their torturers often said to give them false hope. Hope they would not be hurt or killed.

"What are ye saying?" Duncan could not believe the words from his former friend's mouth.

Farlan came close, nose to nose with him. "I said, beg."

"Ye are mad," Duncan replied and stumbled sideways when Farlan struck him hard on the side of the head.

Before he could recover, Farlan raised the large stone he'd hidden in his hand and hit him again.

MOVEMENT COMPOUNDED THE throbbing in his temples. Duncan struggled against the binds at his wrists and ankles. He was gagged so it was impossible to call for help. With each pull, his legs rose from the ground higher and higher, and he realized Farlan was pulling him to hang upside down.

His sword remained strapped to his back, but it was impossible to reach it bound as he was.

After several tries to say something, he gave up as his voice was barely audible. If Caelan was out looking for him along with the guards, there was a possibility they'd find him. He'd been careless to think that Farlan only wanted to talk, or to perhaps ask for work.

He turned his head to search for his mount. It was not visible, but it did not mean Farlan had not tethered it to a tree nearby. The horse was his only hope. The animal was not trusting of strangers, which would have made it difficult for Farlan to get to him. Once again, he scanned the area, but the only horse visible was Farlan's.

It took quite a long time for the man to finally have him upside down, his head just a short distance from the ground. Farlan sat next to a tree a short distance away regaining his breath from the exertion.

Duncan was muscular and tall; his weight could not have been easy to pull up. And yet here he was, in a predicament that made him shake with fury. Of all the people who should sympathize with him, it should be Farlan.

It was a long moment before Farlan stood and walked closer. "I know what ye are thinking, of all people ye never considered that I would do something like this. But ye should understand. It was because of ye that I am no longer fully a man." Lowering to his haunches, Farlan's crazed gaze met his. "We were closer than friends. I loved ye."

Duncan's eyes widened. Was it possible that this man had fallen in love with him? Whatever interactions they had, had never been physical. If Farlan's feelings had grown to the point of love, then it made his misguided actions clearer. He wished to alienate Beatrice by making up a past relationship, and now he was taking vengeance like a scorned lover.

A dagger flashed when Farlan held it up to Duncan's face. "Unlike the others, ye can withstand pain. Ye will not cry out, nor will ye care what I do to ye physically."

Duncan glared at him.

"I will watch ye bleed out. Watch yer life ebb as ye realize what all ye are losing. I believe that will hurt ye more than pain."

A sob escaped and Farlan began to cry. "All I wanted was for us to be together. To find happiness somewhere away from people. Why did ye abandon me?" he cried out and sunk the knife into Duncan's side.

It wasn't too painful. Then again, he was used to pain. What worried him was the blood loss. Mentally he wondered if he would bleed more or less by being suspended upside down.

Warm trails of blood traveled down his body until dripping onto the ground. The smell of it took him back to captivity.

The last smack of the whip barely registered. He was half-crazed with pain already and too hoarse to cry out. Laughter rang out when someone cut the rope that bound him to the pole, and he slipped on his own blood falling face-first into the red pool.

A bucket of salty water splashed over him, the water burning his skin to the point of agony as he attempted to crawl away. But he was grabbed by the ankles and dragged back.

Once again, another bucket was poured over him, and he howled with pain. Someone pushed rags into his hands. "Limpia." Clean. They wanted him to clean the deck.

Seeming to no longer find him entertaining, the men walked away, except for one. An old man who always took pity on him. The man neared and helped him to sit. "Do what they said."

"I did…not under…stand," Duncan replied past chattering teeth. "I tried to do it. I-I tried to."

Tears flowed down his face at the injustice of his life. They'd wanted him to beat another man who'd been tied to the post with one hand. But the man was healthy and fit and had beat Duncan easily.

The older man looked around, pulled a piece of dry flatbread from his shirt, and gave it to Duncan. Once he gobbled it down, the man brought him ale. "Drink, pronto."

Once he ate, they cleaned the deck. The old man did most of the work since Duncan could barely move without crying out in pain. When they were done, the man motioned for him to follow back to his cell.

"Can I watch the sky for a few moments?" Duncan asked pointing to the sky.

"Si. Un momento."

Duncan lifted himself to sit on an upturned barrel and looked across the expanse of the sea. He had no idea where he was or how long he'd been gone. The old man, who was the only one to speak a bit of English, did not know enough to tell him the date.

For a long moment he stared at the sky, taking in the clouds floating in the blue expanse.

"Vamos," the old man said and walked him down the stairs where he would remain forgotten, and perhaps not fed for days.

Once he sat in the cell, the old man handed him a small sack and a wineskin.

Inside the sack were two pieces of flatbread and some dry meat. He didn't bother to see what the wineskin had because all he could do was shake from pain.

He lay on a layer of rags he'd collected each time he cleaned and prayed that he would be rescued soon.

Duncan looked to Farlan, who seemed to be mesmerized by the blood. The blade sliced through the fabric of his tunic. For a long time Farlan inspected his bare chest and ran a hand down from his stomach to between his chest muscles.

Unfocused eyes slid to meet his. "Ye stopped bleeding," he stated matter-of-factly.

When he stuck the dagger into the same wound, this time it hurt a great deal and Duncan moaned. The sound seemed to take Farlan aback because he stumbled backward. "It hurt?"

It was as if he'd truly not expected him to feel anything. Rounded eyes traveled from his wound to his face. And he hurried over and untied his gag.

"Even if I was able to rescue ye, there would have never been anything between us. I did not feel the same about ye," Duncan said, his voice hoarse from the gag. "Cut me down Farlan. Stop this."

"No!" Farlan yelled. "I will finish it. I must."

"Ye do not have to. We could continue our friendship. Ye could work on my lands."

Farlan's eyes narrowed. "Ye would do that?"

"I would," Duncan said. "Please let me down." It was becoming harder to breathe and his head hurt.

The man walked in a circle, murmuring. "I cannot. It is too

late. Ye know how I feel and will hold it over me. No. I could never."

Farlan whirled toward Duncan. "Ye are trying to trick me. Once I cut ye down, ye planned to cut me through." He held up the dagger as tears flowed down his face. "I am sorry. Ye have to die now."

He took only one step and then suddenly froze, his eyes widening.

It was then Duncan saw the arrow lodged through his neck. A second arrow impaled itself straight into Farlan's heart.

The man fell face-first to the ground.

Duncan didn't have to see who it was to know it would be Stuart who rushed into the clearing. A moment later a huge warhorse appeared, its giant hooves running over Farlan's corpse as his brother neared and jumped from the beast before it came to a stop.

His brother met his gaze and Duncan grimaced. "Do ye plan to admire me all day or cut me down?"

"Ye're a bloody mess," Stuart said and let out a shrill whistle, then a second one.

Moments later, three additional horsemen joined Stuart. Gideon, Ewan, and Darach, each on warhorses entered the clearing, the giant beasts pawing the ground sensing their rider's moods.

Darach and Ewan held Duncan still as Gideon climbed onto Stuart's shoulders and cut the rope. They lowered him to the ground with hands on his shoulders to keep him from getting up too fast.

As sensation came to his feet, Duncan grunted. "I do not

think I can walk right now."

"Who is that man?" Darach said looking to where Farlan lay.

"He and I were captives together. We'd promised if one of us escaped, we would return for the other."

"So, the mad man was angry because ye did not rescue him," Stuart stated matter-of-factly.

Duncan nodded refusing to look in the direction of the dead man. "He must be buried."

"I will send the guards to do it," Darach said. "They were ordered to remain at the house to guard it as we didn't know what exactly occurred."

Gideon and Ewan pulled Duncan up to sit. His wound ached but felt much better when Gideon wrapped his midsection tightly with strips and tied them into place.

"I require a tunic. I do not wish for Beatrice to see…" He couldn't finish the sentence, but if anyone understood it was his brothers, who'd all sat and listened to him talk when he'd returned home.

"Take mine," Stuart said, pulling his tunic off over his head and then helping Duncan put it on.

"When will our family have peace?" Gideon asked glaring at the body. "We deserve to have a life without strife. At least for a short while." Their father, who'd been a tyrant, had only been dead a bit over a year. They were still recovering from the ramifications of decisions he'd made. After a threat of battle from another clan, now Duncan had almost been killed.

Darach shook his head. "We can wish for the moon, but the wishes will not make it come down to us."

"DARLING, ARE YE awake?" Beatrice's face hovered over him and Duncan did his best to smile. He wanted to reassure her despite the fact something dark had awakened inside of him.

There was no need to burden Beatrice with it. What good would it do? He'd fought the constant war that waged inside him—barely winning. Now it seemed inevitable that he would not conquer it.

She inspected the bandage around his waist, her pretty face marred by a worried frown. "At least it is not bleeding now."

Tears flowed down her face as she met his gaze. "I do not know what I would have done if ye would have been killed."

"I am very much alive," he cupped her face with both hands and wiped at her tears with his thumbs. "Do not cry."

Beatrice huffed. "If he were not already dead, I would kill the idiot myself. And to think I invited him here."

When Duncan pulled his wife against his chest, it was to keep her from seeing anything in his gaze. At the moment, he wasn't sure what to do, how to feel, or what to think. His head whirled with memories that he'd thought to have shoved away.

"Duncan?"

"Yes?"

"Do ye wish to talk about it?"

"No, I do not."

CHAPTER FOURTEEN

Tense with anticipation, Beatrice leaned forward the entire ride to Keep Ross. Her mother would arrive that day. A messenger had been dispatched with the news as soon as the birlinns were spotted by guardsmen.

"We will go directly to the shore to greet them," Duncan repeated. Seated across from her, he didn't seem at all nervous about what would happen when her family arrived. For all she knew both Evander and Padraig would arrive and draw their swords upon first laying eyes upon Duncan.

In her letter, she'd done her best to explain that the marriage happened because of extraneous circumstances that she'd caused. However, her eldest brother was not only hot-tempered but would probably not believe her.

She silently prayed that it was Padraig and not Evander who arrived, since the youngest had a bit less of a hot temperament.

Freshly bathed, with his hair tied back and tunic open at the neck, her husband was enticing. Beatrice allowed her gaze to linger down his body recalling that just the night before she'd found delight pressed against it.

"Should ye be undressing me at this moment?" Duncan asked with a lift to the corner of his lips.

Beatrice gasped. "I am doing no such thing." The warming

of her cheeks was proof that she lied, so she lifted her eyes to his. "I am fortunate to have ye for a husband. Ye are very handsome."

It was endearing that his face brightened at the compliment, but he then shrugged it off as if it were nothing. "It is I who is most fortunate Beatrice."

Her chest constricted at his warm regard, while at the same time she wondered how he truly felt about her. Would he ever love her?

One of the things she looked forward to, was discussing how love felt. They'd not been visited since marrying, as it was her family custom for a newly married couple to be together for a fortnight. Since the marriage had been hasty and without more than a day's notice, Beatrice had not held Duncan to it. However, they had spent most of the time together.

She glanced at his mid-section that was healing nicely from the wound. "Do not forget, it has not been long enough for ye to ride. I know ye enjoy such things with yer brothers, but it would not be good if ye fall from yer steed."

"I am healed."

She placed a hand on his knee. "Ye are not."

The sounds of horses and voices made Beatrice whirl toward the window. Several people, as well as carriages, guardsmen, and nosy villagers, had gathered.

It was a busy day for arrivals, it seemed. Two bìrlinns neared the shore, the passengers helped to disembark. Immediately, people rushed to greet the travelers, while Beatrice watched from the carriage.

"There is my sister and Ella. I must go to them." Beatrice opened the door and was assisted down by the coachman.

As soon as they noticed her, both women hurried to greet her, and they hugged exclaiming happily.

"Where is Lady Mariel?" Beatrice asked.

"At Ewan's. Visiting Catriona and the bairns. I am sure she will arrive at the keep soon upon learning yer mother arrives," Ella explained.

Beatrice grimaced. "It will not help things that she is not here to help calm Mother."

Her sister nodded. "I just told Ella the same thing. The only good thing is that she will not make a scene in public."

"I am so very anxious," Beatrice said with a shiver. "Mother will be so angry."

Isobel hugged her again. "The preparations for the festivities are all in place. Ye will love what we have prepared."

"I cannot believe that I wasn't part of the planning," Beatrice replied with a pout. "I would have enjoyed it tremendously.

"Aye, I know," Isobel said, her eyes bright with excitement. "I chose every detail with yer tastes in mind."

"I know ye made it perfect," Beatrice said. "I almost came to see what was being done, but I spent the last week caring for Duncan."

Ella shook her head. "My brothers certainly know how to ruin the first days of marriage."

"It was not his fault," Beatrice said.

"My brothers seem to attract conflict at times. If not because they caused it, then because of circumstances they find themselves in."

The Macdonald bìrlinns came into view and they stopped speaking to watch.

"Evander's temperament causes many a conflict," Isobel said tracking the movements of the birlinns. "I wonder at times if he enjoys it."

Once the birlinns were pulled ashore, the three women hurried forward to greet Lady Macdonald.

Their mother's sharp gaze went immediately to Beatrice, taking her in fully before moving to Isobel. Her *I am not happy with either of ye* look was sent out to encompass them both.

Isobel greeted her mother first, kissing her cheeks. "I have missed ye so." Honey dripped from each word and Beatrice fought not to giggle.

Goodness, her nerves were making it hard to figure out what to say. She neared and did what Isobel had just done, kissing her cheeks. "Mother... I am glad ye are here."

"Are ye?" Lady Macdonald's right eyebrow rose high. "I am doubtful."

"Welcome Lady Macdonald," Ella said with a curtsy just as Darach neared. The laird greeted her mother warmly and asked who'd traveled with her.

It was then the entire group turned to the birlinn. After helping drag the vessel to shore and speaking to the men who were to remain with it, Evander Macdonald lifted a huge trunk and carried it to a wagon where he placed it. He then returned to gather a second one.

"Yer belongings," Lady Macdonald said sliding a glance to Beatrice. "Ye have too many things."

Astonished, Beatrice remained silent as trunk after trunk was loaded, then another wagon was brought to be loaded as well.

"That is all mine?" she asked wide-eyed.

"Oh, Beatrice," her mother snapped. "Of course not, some things belong to Isobel. It is not all about ye."

Isobel slid Beatrice a look, and she didn't dare say another word.

"We should go to the carriage. We shall ride together so we can chat about the upcoming festivities." Poor Ella did her best to pretend there wasn't any tension in the air.

Her mother turned to Ella and kissed her cheek. "Ye are a dear girl."

As they made their way to the carriage, Beatrice wondered if she should go with Duncan to keep him from arguing with her brother.

However, they were quickly pushed into the carriage and were headed to Keep Ross before she could think coherently.

"What festivities?" Her mother asked Ella, whom she decided was the only one worthy of her attention at the moment.

Ella smiled warmly. "We were waiting for ye to celebrate Beatrice and Duncan's marriage."

Instantly her mother's icy glare slid to Beatrice, who sat across from her. "I see."

"We have invited minstrels, and a poet..." Isobel began only to stop speaking when their mother turned to Ella.

"Am I right to assume vows have been exchanged and not just a handfasting?"

"A handfasting would have been good enough," Beatrice replied at this point becoming too angry to care if her mother did not speak directly to her. "However, we had little choice as the storm brought attention to our being forced to spend a night alone in an abandoned, dirty, cold building."

"What about yer mother?" Lady Macdonald asked Ella.

"Where is she?"

Ella beamed, seeming to enjoy the fact Beatrice and Isobel were in trouble. "She should be at the keep by the time we arrive. She was at Ewan and Catriona's home. Now that she is a grandmother, she is often there to see the bairns."

Her mother's face finally softened making Beatrice wish she was with child. It would make things easier. It was too soon to know as she was due to start her monthly courses any day.

Once they were well on their way, her mother asked about her home and about what help she had available. Lady Macdonald was very interested in the distance between where she lived and Isobel's home and was glad to hear it was less than a day's ride.

Upon entering the gates, her mother beamed when seeing Lady Mariel and demanded to be assisted down immediately. She hurried to her friend and they disappeared into the house.

"Goodness," Isobel said. "I am sure we have not heard the last of it."

"Ye are correct," Beatrice replied. "Now please help me to ensure Evander does not try to start a fight with Duncan. Our brother is a well-proportioned man, but Duncan is huge and very strong. I would hate for Evander to spend his time here recovering."

Carts with the trunks entered the gates, followed by her and Duncan's carriage, and finally by Duncan and Evander, who frowned in her direction.

"He does not look especially angry," Isobel remarked.

"How can ye tell?" Ella asked studying Evander, whose light brown hair glimmered in the sunlight.

Beatrice giggled. "Because he is not yelling and hitting things."

"I am sure he is not that horrible," Ella replied. "He seems a bit annoyed, but I would not say angry."

Her sister huffed. "How about ye be the one responsible for showing him his bedchamber. Come, sister." Isobel grabbed her arm and they raced into the house and directly to the kitchen. "It is best to avoid him until Darach speaks to him about what has occurred."

"I really should check on Duncan," Beatrice said. "He could tear open his wound."

"If he hurts himself while tossing Evander across the room, I will help ye tend to him," Isobel remarked. "Our brother needs to learn to keep his temper in check."

"I agree," Beatrice said and sat down across the table in a small room that was usually reserved for the servants.

Her sister studied her for a moment. "Ye look well. How does marriage suit ye?"

She had so many questions and so many things she wanted to speak to Isobel about. But it wasn't the time or the place.

Instead, she just said. "I am enjoying settling into our home and we are both getting to know one another. I still have much to learn about... things."

"Me as well," Isobel said. "Give yerself time."

"I hired a chambermaid. It is a widow and her son, who is about ten and five. They have been a huge help. We have decided to keep the staff small, as there are only three of us there most days."

"That must be an adjustment," Isobel said. "We both grew up in a place like this with people constantly about."

Gideon entered the kitchen and Beatrice called out to him. Upon entering, Beatrice motioned to a chair. "Please tell me what is happening between my brother and Duncan."

"Ye can see them outside through the kitchen window," Gideon said walking back to the kitchen.

Both she and Isobel raced to the door instead.

Like two cocks preparing to fight to the death, Duncan and Evander circled each other while speaking at each other in the short hard sentences of angry men.

"Should we go and stop them?" Beatrice asked, unable to look away.

Isobel shook her head. "Darach and Stuart are there. Hopefully one of them will intercede if it comes to blows."

"I hope not," Beatrice said and walked out, Isobel following.

Gideon came and stood next to them. "Do not interfere. This is something they must work out between them. Evander said something offensive to Duncan, my brother has to decide how to proceed."

"It looks as if they have decided to proceed in the worst way," Isobel said in a low angry tone. "Violence does not solve anything."

Beatrice tugged at Gideon's arm. "Duncan is injured. I am not sure his wound has healed properly."

"Duncan outweighs yer brother and is taller."

"That does not make me feel better in the least," Beatrice snapped.

Thankfully Darach walked between the men and said something in low tones. Both Duncan and Evander looked to the doorway where their mothers stood. Each one with a furious expression.

"If anything will ruin a good fight, it is our mother's watching," Gideon grumbled and walked away.

While Ella took Evander to show him his room, Beatrice went to Duncan. "Let us rest before last meal," she said peering up at him. "It has been a long day already."

He nodded. "First, ye and Isobel need to divide yer belongings so the driver can take yers to our house."

While she went to the wagons and instructed the men on which would go to her home and which would stay, Duncan stood nearby. He was silent, his arms crossed and attention toward the stables. Inside the sounds of conversations rose as people gathered for last meal.

With all that had happened, along with her mother's arrival and Evander's reaction, she'd not considered that Duncan had a hard time with large gatherings. His own sister planned the festivities, had Ella not taken Duncan into consideration?

She'd have to ask. When all the items that were for their home were loaded onto a single wagon, Duncan instructed the driver along with a guard to return to their home with the items and to ask Gara to oversee where they were to be placed.

When he came to her and turned toward the house, Beatrice stopped him by placing her hand on his forearm. "If ye wish to return to the house for now and return later for the celebration I understand. I know ye do not like large gatherings."

The muscle in his jaw flexed, a sign she recognized that showed he was annoyed. "It is not that I do not like gatherings. It is that..." He stopped talking because Ella emerged from the house and hurried over.

"Darach has Evander in the study and wishes for ye to join them." She gave him a knowing look. "He said to take yer time."

Again, the muscle flexed, and Ella caught sight of it. "Come, Beatrice, let us give Duncan a few moments."

"He is angry," Beatrice said not expecting a reply. "Do ye think it may be best for him to return to the house for a day?"

"No," Ella replied. "He will be fine. Duncan is slow to anger and slow to calm as well."

"I am beginning to understand him." When they walked into the great room, the women were in the dining room away from the noise.

From the smile on her mother's face, Lady Mariel had helped calm her. However, upon seeing Beatrice, she bristled. "I have yet to speak to ye about yer rash actions."

"Isobel was quite thorough in giving me a tongue thrashing. I am so embarrassed by my actions and the position that I forced Duncan, Darach, and both of ye into," Beatrice said to the table. "It was not my intention at all and for it, I am truly sorry." She blinked back tears. "It had always been my dream to marry with ye, Father, and Padraig present and that Evander give me away."

To her horror, her mother wiped tears away. "That is what hurt me the most. I know we cannot always control what fate brings. I should have sent one of yer brothers to fetch ye immediately."

"Are they suited?" her mother asked Lady Mariel who shrugged in return. "They went to the other house upon marrying and I have not had occasion to see them interact yet. I suppose we will learn together."

The mothers turned to Beatrice and she felt her cheeks redden.

Before she could answer, Duncan entered the room. He'd obviously come straight from outside. He went to the head of the table and lowered over her mother's hand placing a kiss to the back of it. "Lady Aileen, I am glad that ye arrived without incident and that ye are here to spend time with us and with my family. Please do us the pleasure of coming to stay at our home for a few days."

Her mother blushed at Duncan's attentions. "I suppose it would be good for me to see how ye live."

"We get along very well Mother," Beatrice said smiling at Duncan. "We are well suited."

Duncan came to where Beatrice sat and placed a kiss on her temple. "I will be at Darach's study if ye require anything."

Her mother followed his movement as he walked out of the house. "He is such a large man."

"My son is a good man, who was dealt a horrible hand. Yet despite it, he is fair, kind, and gentle. The most innocent of the lot."

Ella laughed. "He is indeed. The only one that was rarely scolded by Mother as a lad."

When Greer and several servants appeared with something to hold them until last meal, her mother informed them of all the happenings in North Uist. She told them of the MacNeil's visit and of how bothersome Lady MacNeil was.

As Beatrice listened to her talk about her father, she asked many questions. "As soon as we can, Duncan and I must go see Father. I miss him dearly."

"He sent a missive to Darach about it. Yer father expects

that ye and Duncan will travel to North Uist to spend the winter season with us. The only reason Isobel and Darach are not included in this is because of his duties as laird."

Isobel sighed. "I would not mind going. I will discuss it with Darach. Perhaps he can hand the reins of lairdship to Stuart for winter."

Their mother clapped with glee. "That would be delightful. It would make yer father very happy."

Ella and her mother exchanged concerned glances and Beatrice wondered if it had to do with Darach or Duncan leaving for so long.

Once they finished eating, Beatrice went to the stairs and stopped. Would she and Duncan be staying in the same room?

Perhaps it was time to admit to him that she'd seen his body and knew every scar on it. The last thing she needed at that moment was for him to demand separate bedchambers when being scrutinized by both her mother and Evander.

CHAPTER FIFTEEN

"I T IS A gesture of goodwill that Laird Macdonald invites ye and Beatrice go to North Uist," Darach said. "Of course, ye must go."

They sat around a table in Darach's study. The room was cavernous and without a window and despite preferring the same for his own bedchamber, Duncan found this room oppressive. Perhaps it was because it had been his father's prior to Darach's. With the attention on him now, he had a strong urge to get up and leave.

Duncan remained silent, not wishing to say anything else to anger Beatrice's brother, whose narrowed gaze was locked on him.

They would expect him to share a bedchamber with her. His needing time away from her and everyone else could prove to be a great insult. Yet Duncan knew he could not turn the invitation down, not unless he could come up with a good reason for it. In that moment nothing came to mind.

"I wish to speak to ye in private," Evander said. "Just talk," he said when Darach began to say something. "No fists or swords involved."

With a nod, Darach met his gaze. A firm message to remain calm in the look his brother gave him.

Very well, Duncan stood and walked across the hall to the

parlor where he and Beatrice had their first conversation. The irony was not lost on him. Evander followed at a distance. Finally, both went to stand by the windows that overlooked the seashore.

"What do ye wish to talk about?" Duncan said, not wanting to prolong things longer than necessary.

Evander looked out to the view, much like his sister had. Duncan studied the man's profile. The fact his nose looked to be broken fit the description Beatrice gave him: hot-tempered. And when young—brash and headstrong.

"I know quite a bit about ye," Evander began, the words surprising him. "That ye were a captive for many years."

Releasing a long breath, Duncan remained silent waiting to hear what Evander had to say.

The man's bi-colored gaze locked with his. "Will yer past affect how ye treat my sister?"

The question was valid and yet it angered Duncan. How long would he carry the past on his back like a heavy stone? Forever he guessed. "I would never allow my past to affect my marriage. I have never nor will I ever mistreat a woman. I care for Beatrice, her well-being is the most important thing in the world to me. I would lay down my life for her."

"What ye feel and what could happen are very different things. I know men who have had experiences like yers and are harmful. Not all intentionally."

A person would believe what they wished, and he had no intention of trying to change Evander's mind. So, he shrugged. "I can only speak to the years since my release."

"Does Beatrice know everything?"

"That I was whipped so many times, there isn't an inch of

my body without a scar? Or that I was forced to kill men with my bare hands? Should I inform her of the times I begged for death to claim me? I am sure she needs to know that there are men who pay to watch grown men suffer. To be raped and to be broken down until they cry like children."

Evander looked to the floor. "I am sorry. I did not mean…"

"She knows that I was held captive. I keep the scars hidden, as much as I can. There is no need for her to know the extent of the depravity of some men."

"I agree," Evander replied. There was respect in his eyes when looking at him and he held out his hand. "All I wish is for both of my sisters to be treated well and protected."

"She is and will always be safe. Ye have my word," Duncan said meaning it, and took Evander's extended hand.

There was a soft knock and a servant walked in. "Last meal is about to be served."

Duncan showed Evander to the dining room and took his seat next to Beatrice who gave him a questioning look.

"I will explain later," he whispered into her ear.

All his brothers, except for Caelan, who planned to arrive the next day attended last meal. The women mostly spoke to Ewan's wife Catriona about the newly born boy, while his brothers found out that Evander was an avid hunter and began to talk of planning a hunt.

For the most part he remained quiet, listening to the conversations. Duncan realized Evander had not demanded a reply to the Macdonald's invitation. Perhaps he would be more understanding of him not wishing to go.

Separate bedchambers had allowed him to protect Beatrice

from overhearing anything during his horrible dreams and from accidentally seeing his scars.

If he declined, it would hurt her and he hated it, but going to another place for an entire season terrified him.

"Are ye not hungry?" Beatrice asked with an incredulous expression. She was aware he loved Greer's cooking.

"I am," he said picking up the meat and biting into it.

Thankfully, the conversation drew her back in and she stopped paying attention to him. Duncan felt someone watching and looked up to meet Darach's gaze. His brother looked to his mother and back to him.

Duncan listened to what was being said. Apparently, his mother planned to join him and Beatrice for a season in North Uist, along with Darach and Isobel.

What was Darach thinking? Had his brother gone daft from being in love and not considered that an entire season was too long for both eldest brothers to be gone from Keep Ross?

Stuart and Gideon joined in the conversation seeming to agree that due to the cold weather, there would be little trouble. If they planned and ensured the people had food stock and any repairs done to the homes, there was no impediment to them going.

Duncan pushed from the table and walked out without looking back.

At first, he thought the wind howled in his ears, however, it was his own heartbeat. It had been a trying day, filled with too many people and too much conversation. Then there was the consensus of those in his family that he should travel to see the Macdonald.

As if he'd ever been part of such a party. The only time he'd traveled with a group and stayed in close quarters was when he was a captive and that was out of his control. This was not.

"Duncan," Beatrice walked to him. It bothered him that she approached with caution, measuring her steps. "I am sorry about my brother. I know he can be hot-tempered…"

A part of him wanted to crush her against him, at the same time the urge to mount and leave was just as strong. Perhaps even stronger.

He was about to do exactly that, he realized, looking over his shoulder to see he stood next to the horse corral.

"I needed air," he explained. "Too many people and conversation. I am not angry at yer brother. He has a right to demand an explanation and question me about ye."

Beatrice bit her bottom lip, the action making him want to kiss the moistened morsel when she released it. "I have to admit, I was more worried about him than ye. Ye are so much larger." She giggled. "I had a vision of ye throwing him across the courtyard, much like a heavy stone or a caber."

"The idea occurred to me when he wouldn't listen," Duncan admitted. "But I would not do anything so violent, especially not in front of ye."

She rushed to him and wrapped her arms around his midsection, her head against the center of Duncan's chest. "Ye are a good man, husband."

Beatrice was like a balm to his troubled soul, a soothing elixir that seeped through the layers of scarring, making him feel like a normal man.

Pulling her tight, he pressed a kiss to the top of her head.

"Is yer mother cross with ye?"

"Very much so. She is somewhat soothed with the idea of a wedding celebration. But I foresee a private scolding in my immediate future. I am sure she and Evander have much to say."

"Would ye like me to be present?"

She lifted her face up to his and Duncan kissed her lightly.

"Nay. I know what they will say, and they will be correct in their anger that I acted without thought. My impulsiveness has gotten me into situations in the past. None with such broad consequences."

Duncan placed his finger under her chin lifting her face. "In this instance, I am glad of the consequences."

Her smile brightened his mood. "I admit to enjoying the result of my actions very much."

As if his manhood had ears, it began to harden. Beatrice must have sensed his arousal because she rubbed her hands up and down his back. If only it were possible for her to touch his skin.

"We should return indoors. It may be best for ye to face them now and get it over with."

"True," Beatrice replied. "Tomorrow the wedding celebration begins. Did ye remember to bring yer tartan and crest?"

As they walked back toward the house, his wife listed everything he should have brought as he replied, "aye" and nodded. It was a normal moment in a marriage that Duncan treasured. When she frowned up at him, he smiled.

"Duncan, I am serious. Ye must see about getting yer haircut. Just a bit, not too much. I prefer it long."

"I will see to it now. Greer cuts it for me."

"Very well," she eyed him critically. "Oh, and ye should see about yer beard as well."

He nodded enjoying her fussing over him and his appearance. When she took his hand and inspected his fingernails, he wanted to laugh. "I doubt guests will be examining my hands."

"Hmm," Beatrice replied seeming satisfied as she didn't instruct him to cut or clean them.

Before they entered the house, he took her arm and pulled her to a stop.

"What is it?" She looked up at him with wide eyes.

"I care for ye very much and am glad to be here."

Beatrice's face softened, her lips curved, and her beautiful clear blue eyes glistened with happy tears. "Thank ye, I needed to hear that."

NIGHT CAME AND Beatrice paced the room she and Duncan were to share. It would be the first time they would spend the night together. Well, the first night that he would be aware of, since she'd been sneaking into his room and sleeping beside him on the nights, he had nightmares.

Although exhausted, she was nervous at his lack of appearance. She'd gone to the door several times to search for him but decided it was best to allow Duncan the time he needed.

Finally, Duncan entered; his gaze meeting hers before going to the bed. "I thought ye'd be asleep by now."

A retort was on the tip of her tongue. Instead, she removed her robe, went to the bed, and slipped between the blankets. "I am very tired, but I wished to tell ye about the discussion with

Mother and Evander."

After removing his boots and breeches, Duncan went to the washstand and washed his face, hands, and between his legs. Once that was completed, he came to the bed wearing a soft tunic that he often wore when coming to her bedchamber. He never removed it unless there was no light in the room.

As Beatrice spoke, he listened intently, lying on his back looking up at the ceiling. He acknowledged what she said and agreed when she was indignant. When Beatrice looked at him, he was having a hard time keeping his eyes open.

She pressed a kiss to his jaw. "Sleep well."

A sound awakened her, and Beatrice reached for Duncan's side of the bed. He had his back to her and was murmuring in his sleep. It pained her that he seemed to have such vivid, disturbing dreams every night.

Ever so slowly, she reached for him and ran her hand down his arm. When he quieted, she snuggled against his back and he let out a soft sigh. Through the thin fabric Beatrice could feel the raised scarring, the ridges and bumps resulting from his torture. They were a part of her husband and she embraced their existence.

Dawn came too soon. Beatrice woke to find herself still against Duncan, seeking warmth from the chilly room.

He slept soundly and she took advantage and snuggled closer letting out a content sigh. She knew immediately when he woke because his body tensed.

Beatrice pretended to sleep to see what he would do. At first, he attempted to slip away, but with her arm around his waist he couldn't move. Then he lifted her arm, but she mumbled sleepily and snuggled even closer.

Finally, he gave up, surrendering to the fact it would be impossible to get out of her embrace unless he slipped out of the bed.

"Ye are funny," Beatrice murmured with a soft chuckle. "I wondered if ye would figure out how to escape or give up."

He grunted and rolled to his back, pulling her against his side. Emboldened by him not moving away, Beatrice reached between his legs and was pleasantly surprised to find him fully aroused.

His breath caught and he let out a sharp hiss. "Men wake up hard," he grunted out by way of explanation.

"It is not a bad thing." Beatrice slid her hand up and down the hardened shaft. "Is it?"

"I suppose not," he rolled over her. "Ye want me?"

"Very much so."

Beatrice tugged at his tunic, but he pulled her hands up above her head. When she squirmed, he took her mouth, kissing her breathless, the entire time his sex sliding between hers, but not entering her.

The friction of what he did made her need even greater, and she pulled away from his kisses. "Duncan, please. Take me."

Still holding her hands, but now in just one of his, he reached between them and guided himself. With one thrust, he filled her completely and both cried out at the wonderful overwhelming of the senses.

Pulling out and driving back into her, Duncan set a controlled pace. Needing him deeper, Beatrice wrapped her legs around his waist.

To her delight, he released her hands to slip his under her

bottom, lifting it off the bed as he continued to plunge, faster and faster, sending them spiraling out of control.

Beatrice cried out blindly as she clutched his shoulders, her fingernails digging through the fabric into his flesh, not wishing to lose herself totally. But it did little to stifle the passion that overtook.

"Oh. Oh. Oh," she said over and over, needing to verbalize but at the same time unable to form coherent words.

Duncan's intense expression was a beautiful sight. The cords of his neck protruding as he strained to maintain the pace. His gaze met hers for a moment, and she became lost in his eyes, but soon lost focus when he rolled over so that she straddled him.

For a moment, she was unsure what to do, but instinct took over and she pressed her palms on his chest and allowed him to guide her.

It was a delightful change that brought different sensations. Beatrice used her thighs, riding her husband steadily, reveling in having control of their lovemaking.

His gaze trailed down the length of her body and he touched a spot that brought sharp sensations with each caress. Beatrice lost the rhythm of her movements, her eyes widening when he rubbed the nub at the top of her sex between his fingers.

She shook with a release so hard, a loud cry erupted.

As she trembled from the aftereffects, Duncan took her by the hips and used her body to bring himself to release. His entire large body shook so hard, Beatrice climaxed once again.

"Do ye think someone overheard us?" Beatrice whispered when she finally could.

"If they did not, they are deaf," Duncan replied as if discussing the weather.

Beatrice sat up alarmed. "Oh, goodness. This is mortifying."

"We are newly married. It is expected that we enjoy bedsport." His matter-of-fact tone earned him a smack on the chest from her.

"It may be something to boast about for men. But it is believed women should not enjoy it."

"Ye can pretend to be offended," he replied. From the curve to his lips, her husband was quite proud of his accomplishment.

Beatrice slipped from the bed and poured water into the basin to wash up. "We should dress. First meal must already be started. Hopefully, they had all gone downstairs and were not about to overhear."

By the way everyone in the dining room avoided looking directly at her and the discreet glances between the men, most at the table had indeed either overheard them or those that did not had been informed of it.

"Ye are late to rise this morning," her oblivious mother stated.

There were grunts and clearing of throats around the table as Duncan's brothers attempted to keep from laughing. Beatrice glared at Gideon, who sat across from her. It had little effect.

Isobel nudged Beatrice with her leg. "There is much to do today to prepare for the celebration."

"Some celebrating has already begun," Ella said with a wide grin. Lady Mariel shook her head giving Ella a warning look.

"Other than some decorating, there is little left to be done. The clan's people who come to seek counsel from Darach will be sent to the parlor so we can keep the great hall empty until it is time."

"I cannot wait for ye to see the dress I brought," her mother exclaimed, and Beatrice clapped. "I just know it will be beautiful. Thank ye, Mother."

"It is a special day and I want ye to enjoy it thoroughly."

When Duncan and Stuart exchanged a look, Beatrice pinched Duncan's leg under the table.

He gave her a surprised look and whispered in her ear, "That hurt."

"Ye will live," she replied dryly.

Evander glared at them.

CHAPTER SIXTEEN

T HE CELEBRATION WAS wonderful. Lavender sprays had been layered with greenery down the center of the long tables in the great hall. Candlelight from every space gave a magical appearance and the lively music made for a most wonderfully perfect gathering.

Her gown was a beautiful creation of cream and soft green that flowed with every movement.

When a familiar song played, everyone began singing. Some looking to her and Duncan as it was customary for the bride and groom to dance.

To her surprise, Duncan stood and took her hand. He led her down from the sideboard to the open area for dancing. His left arm circled her waist and with his right, he took her hand. Then they danced, circling the entire area. Although it was obvious he was not used to dancing and their movements were not perfect, it was like a wonderful dream to her.

When she stole a glance to where her mother sat, Lady Macdonald was wiping tears of joy. Beatrice smiled in her direction and her mother gave her a warm look.

At the next song, others joined them as they danced to a second song. However, when the tempo of the music changed to a much livelier tune, Duncan released Beatrice to join the other women who'd joined hands and danced in a circle.

It was one of the most enjoyable days of her life and Beatrice wanted the day to never end.

The room silenced when Darach stood and held up his cup. He turned first to those gathered and then to Beatrice and Duncan.

"I welcome ye, Beatrice Macdonald Ross, to our clan and family. May God grant ye and my brother happiness and long lives. That ye have healthy crops, healthy livestock, and many bairns." The room erupted in cheers and Beatrice laughed.

The next in line by birth order was Caelan, who lifted his cup and met Duncan's gaze. "I wish ye, my brother and closest friend, much happiness with yer beautiful bride. To ye Beatrice, we welcome ye with open arms and open hearts."

As the rest of the brothers spoke, Beatrice had to wipe tears from her eyes. Duncan squeezed her hand when Evander stood.

"I am here as a representative of Clan Macdonald. My father sends his blessings to Beatrice and to ye, Duncan. Our clans are bound by marriage now twice and for that we are thankful; especially since the bond between our mothers has always been strong. We welcome ye, Duncan Ross, to our clan. I wish ye and my sister much happiness. Beatrice, do yer best to stay out of trouble."

Everyone laughed at the last words.

Finally, the night was over, and Duncan carried a sleepy, happy Beatrice up the stairs to their bedchamber.

As they prepared for bed, he once again headed to the bed with his tunic on.

When he reached for a lantern to blow it out, Beatrice stopped him. "Please leave it on. I want to see ye fully bereft of clothing. I so enjoyed seeing yer face this morning when we made love.

He froze, as if unsure how to proceed. Beatrice walked to him as he considered the options.

"I must confess something to ye," Beatrice said quietly. "By now, as ye are aware, I quite often do things without thinking them through. I did something before we married ye should know about."

His gaze bore into hers. "What did ye do?"

"Well," Beatrice bit her bottom lip. "Promise not to be angry"

"Beatrice. I cannot promise without knowing what ye are about to tell me."

"Will ye at least sit then?"

When he sat down, she was surprised that he pulled her onto his lap, his arms loosely around her. "Tell me."

"After Darach demanded we marry, I did not wish for ye to be forced into a marriage against yer will. After coming up with a plan, Ella and I decided to return to North Uist, so I could avoid us being married. Late that night, I snuck down the corridor to come speak to ye. Afraid of being overheard, I did not knock. Instead, I opened the door and came inside while ye slept."

His brow furrowed as he listened. "I did not know. What is so wrong that ye confess to doing it? Obviously, ye did not wake me."

"I did not. But ye were fully naked and had pushed the blankets down to just above yer bum.

Duncan's eyes widened. "Did ye see me?"

"It was a full moon, and as ye know I am very curious,"

Beatrice smiled at him. "Ye have a beautiful body Duncan, I quite enjoyed the view of it."

He visibly swallowed. "Did ye see my front or the back?"

Once again, she bit her lip. "Are ye angry?"

"No." The word however was curt and harsh.

"Ye are angry. I will not continue unless ye admit to it."

"I am not angry. I am troubled."

"Troubled. Very well then, it is not too bad." Beatrice had to admit it all to him. "I had never seen a naked man before, other than catching a glimpse of Padraig once when he bathed in the loch and that was not enjoyable."

Duncan remained tense, his entire attention on her. "Beatrice. Answer me."

Beatrice let out a breath. "I circled yer bed. I am very aware that it is horrible to look upon a sleeping person who is not aware. Even worse, a man I was not married to. And although it makes me sound like a horrible person, I must admit to admiring what I saw that night. Yer back though scarred is so broad and yer bottom, it is perfectly formed. Yer chest and legs..."

To her astonishment, Duncan didn't seem angry. Instead, his eyebrows lifted in surprise. "Ye sound like a man speaking about a woman's body. I have never expected that ye would ogle a man."

"Not just a man. Ye. My husband. I suspect ye tried to hide the scars from me and that is why ye insist on making love in the dark and not allow me to touch ye. Which is why I am telling ye this. I very much want to touch every inch of ye."

"This is the wrong time to be telling me this," he said looking to the doorway. "I am going to kidnap ye and take ye to our house where ye can make all the noise ye wish."

"Tomorrow?" Beatrice teased, pressing a kiss to the side of his mouth. "That is a long time to wait."

The light of the one lantern was enough for her to see clearly as Duncan undressed. His gaze locked with hers for a moment and then he pulled the tunic over his head.

Her breath caught. The man was perfectly made, with a strong sculpted body and long muscled legs.

There was a light sprinkling of hair down the center of his chest that went past his stomach to just above the patch of dark hair over his sex.

At her perusal, his manhood moved, and a shiver went through her.

"Have ye had yer fill of ogling?" Duncan asked with obvious pride in knowing she found him desirable.

"I am not sure I ever will," Beatrice replied. "Ye are beautiful."

"Men are not beautiful," he scoffed nearing the bed. "Can ye not think of another way to describe me?"

"Hmm," she teased pressing a kiss to his shoulder, then trailing her mouth across to press a second one between the mounds of his chest. "Bonnie?"

He pulled her against his chest, his breathing already labored. "I do not wish to continue talking."

When he kissed her, it was as if he'd been waiting for years. His mouth took hers with desperation and want.

Beatrice wrapped her arms around his shoulders and made circular patterns on the back of them. She wanted to explore his entire body, but it would take time. Duncan had undressed before her and that was the first monumental step of many to come.

The feel of his strong body against hers made her shiver with anticipation. "Take me, husband. I need ye desperately."

"Will ye be quiet?" he asked in a soft tone.

"I very much doubt it," Beatrice admitted.

THE NEXT FEW days were like a whirlwind. Her mother insisted on traveling to the village and upon spotting the peddler, spent an exorbitant amount of money purchasing trinkets. After spending three days at Keep Ross, Lady Macdonald was prepared to go to Beatrice and Duncan's home.

Beatrice, her mother, and Orla climbed into the carriage. Lady Mariel, Isobel, and Ella would be visiting the next day. Once they spent a week at their home, they would all prepare to travel to North Uist.

"We cannot delay our return too long," her mother said looking out the window. "Already the weather is turning colder, and very soon it will be impossible to travel."

Beatrice followed her line of sight. "A season will be a long time to remain away from the keep. I am surprised Darach is considering going."

"He has brothers to take his place. What of yer husband? He avoids talk of it."

She'd yet to talk to Duncan about it. "I am sure he is going. Duncan is a private person, who prefers to be away from too many people."

"It is expected that the man who marries a laird's daughter would first seek permission. That did not happen, obviously.

Therefore, it is imperative he meets with yer father to discuss expectations."

"I understand, Mother. As son and brother to lairds, I am sure he is aware of the obligations."

Her mother gave her a dubious look. "How do ye feel about him? Ye seem to enjoy each other's company. I must admit to finding him unapproachable, intimidating even."

"We are getting to know one another, and he is kind and patient with me." Beatrice's lips curved at how hard it had been for them to keep from making noises during sex the night before.

"From the dreamy look on yer face, I ascertained as much and I am glad for it," Her mother smiled. "It settles my mind to know both ye and Isobel have husbands that treat ye well."

Upon arriving at the house, her mother took it in. "It is a grand home, dear."

"It is," Beatrice said. "Very quiet, which I've grown used to."

Evander and Duncan had ridden ahead. Thankfully, after the first day, the two had become somewhat friendly.

BEATRICE WAS EXCITED to entertain and nervous once the others arrived, but thankfully Gara and Firtha handled everything perfectly.

The new chambermaid and her son were kept busy ensuring everyone had all they needed, and by the end of the visit everyone was exhausted.

Duncan let out a long breath as the carriages disappeared

down the road. "I will need a sennight to recover from this."

"We have only three days before leaving for North Uist. Ye may as well make the most of it."

When he didn't reply, Beatrice gave him a sharp look that he didn't meet but instead kept his gaze on the road. With the servants near, she could not question him.

"Are ye going back inside," she asked, turning to the house.

"Nay. I am going for a ride." He walked to the stables, with the long strides of a man in a hurry.

Beatrice narrowed her eyes. Where did he have to be? There was packing to be done and preparations for a long season away.

Annoyed at her reclusive husband, she went back inside. She hurried to find Caelan, who was in his study. As usual, he was impeccably dressed. Upon seeing her, he stood and motioned to a chair. "Ye must be weary with all the meals and entertaining." His gaze was warm. "Ye handled everything perfectly."

"I must admit to being proud," Beatrice replied with a smile. "I came to ask ye something that perplexes me."

"Oh?" Caelan looked to the door. "Should I close the door?"

"Please."

Once he closed the door and settled into a chair next to hers, Beatrice let out a breath. "It is about Duncan."

"I suspected so," Caelan said.

"I am afraid he will not travel to North Uist. My family will not take well to the slight. Each time I bring it up, he remains silent."

"If ye wish, I will speak to him." Caelan met her gaze. "Where is he now?"

For some reason her eyes became watery. "I mentioned that we will be leaving in three days and he did not reply. Then he hurried to the stables, saying he was going for a ride."

Caelan was pensive. "He may be doing it to clear his head and consider the upcoming trip. Duncan understands it is imperative he goes to see yer father. If he is hesitant, there is a good reason for it. Do not worry, I will ensure he clarifies things."

Feeling somewhat better, Beatrice stood. "Thank ye for everything."

Caelan kissed her cheek. "All will be well. Do not fret."

The day progressed quickly, Beatrice and Orla were excited when the seamstress arrived with their dresses. They spent an hour trying them on, while the woman made last-minute adjustments.

When Duncan arrived, Caelan asked to speak to him, and they went back outside. From the great room windows, Beatrice caught glimpses of them. Both seemed calm until Duncan pulled his hair from the plait and raked his fingers through it.

Caelan held up both hands, as if exasperated.

"I wish I could read lips," Beatrice said to Orla, who came to stand next to her. "It seems as if my husband is not happy."

"Neither is Mister Caelan," Orla added.

Duncan paced while talking, while Caelan crossed his arms and leaned on the stone wall.

DURING LAST MEAL, it was as if nothing was out of the ordinary. Duncan was mostly quiet, but that was not unusual, whilst Caelan regaled her with a story about his time away at boarding school.

Beatrice didn't linger after the meal, as she was not in the mood to listen to a conversation about the last game's competition.

Once in her bedchamber, she became annoyed. She and Duncan had not made love in days, mostly because the last two days she'd been too exhausted to remain awake. She'd heard the adjoining door open but hadn't been able to gather the strength to wake fully.

This day, she wasn't as exhausted. The family had left after first meal, leaving the rest of the day to pack some things and she'd even napped.

As she undressed, the adjoining door opened.

A shiver of excitement traveled up her spine and she turned to find Duncan stalking toward her.

He lifted her off the floor, their mouths joined, his tongue immediately probing past her lips. Beatrice lost her breath when he lowered her to the floor and tugged the gown off her shoulders. It slipped down and pooled at her feet.

Between kisses, she helped him remove his clothing until he too stood fully bare before her.

He was magnificent. From his broad shoulders and muscular chest that tapered to slender hips. His thighs were thick and toned from horseback riding. What took her attention was the thick erect shaft between them.

"Ye are perfect," she said trailing her gaze up to meet his gaze. "I need to feel every inch of ye against me." Too excited to wait, she tugged him toward the bed.

Duncan picked her up and placed her on the bed and then climbed in and lay next to her. Facing each other, he ran a hand down her side from under her arm to just below her hip. "I have never seen a more beautiful sight than ye here with me."

It was as if every place his gaze landed came to life, the skin tingled and she shivered in anticipation of what was to come.

She was not disappointed. They made love in a way that was new. Uninhibited, tumbling into different positions until they were breathless and drenched.

Sprawled across Duncan, too spent to move, Beatrice lifted her face and peered up at him. "I believe to have fallen in love with ye," she admitted. "Is it too soon?"

His body quivered and he blew out a breath. "No. It is not. I fell in love with ye a long time ago."

The idea of it gave her strength to climb over him, she looked down at her husband. "And ye did not think I needed to know?"

His lips curved. "Ye are enticing like that."

"Ye annoy me," Beatrice informed him with a playful nip to his bottom lip. "Say it."

"What?"

"Ye know."

"I love ye, Beatrice."

Her heart was filled with so much joy, she expected it to burst. Instead, she began to cry.

"What did I do?" Duncan pulled her against his chest. "Are ye hurt?"

"No," Beatrice said looking up at him. "I am happy. I am crying because I am happy."

THREE DAYS LATER, as the bìrlinns set sail, Beatrice continued to scan the shore hoping to see a horseman arrive. But no one appeared.

"I am sorry," Darach said. "I do not know why my brother left and did not return."

Beatrice blew out a breath to keep the tears at bay. "In my heart, I suspected he would not come. And I cannot forgive him for it."

"Perhaps he will follow. Ye can reprimand him then," Isobel said with a worried look, as she too looked toward the shore.

"No. He will not come. And I will never return."

CHAPTER SEVENTEEN

F OR DAYS HE'D fought to keep the demons at bay. It had been a long time since he'd been so out of control. He'd gone to the forest and ran until his lungs threatened to explode, but still, he could not find it easy to settle.

Since Farlan's appearance, every moment memories haunted him. Each one becoming worse. The lashings in his dreams so real, he felt the pain. So many things he'd forgotten were now so vivid that he wanted to scream and throw himself off a cliff.

Every night after everyone slept, he'd gone outside out of earshot when the visions attacked. He was reduced to howling like a wounded beast.

Beatrice would never forgive him for not going with her.

He'd been planning to go, but at the last moment it proved impossible. And now he was aboard a different birlinn, heading to Skye, away from everyone and everything his life had been.

He'd left a letter for both her and Caelan, and one for Darach, so he could explain things to the family. Not that he expected any of them to begin to understand. How long he would be gone? Duncan wasn't sure. Perhaps forever.

The horse neighed in protest at being tied down and he ran his hand down its long nose. "We are almost there," he soothed, looking into the misty distance.

When they arrived on shore, he paid the fees and mounted. It would be a pair of days travel to arrive where he was headed. Hopefully, the cottage was still there. It would be his home for the foreseeable future.

As he traveled, he imagined Beatrice's disappointment. How he hated hurting her, especially after her falling in love with him. The idea of her feeling pain over his actions made his own ache so much harder to bear.

She must have been devastated.

Duncan let out a frustrated breath. He was so very broken, so lost in his own nightmares that he should have fought harder to keep from marrying her. Instead, he'd been foolish enough to believe it was possible to have a normal life. To grow old with a beautiful wife, raise children, and get to know his grandchildren.

"How stupid of me," he mumbled as night fell and he looked for a place to find shelter and sleep.

THE NEXT DAY, he found the old cottage. To his surprise, Fergus, the old man who lived nearby, hobbled over to greet him.

"Ye promised yerself not to return," he said by way of greeting as he leaned heavily on his cane and watched Duncan dismount.

"There isna much in there. Been empty for a few years." The old man walked to the front door.

With only two cabins in a clearing in the woods, Fergus had appointed himself overseer. When Duncan had stumbled upon the empty cabin ten years earlier, Fergus had found him sick and dirty and with festering wounds. The old man had taken care of him until he'd healed and then promptly found him work and insisted he pay rent.

Duncan had lived there for a year, working and waiting to heal both physically and mentally, before gaining the courage to go home.

"I was foolish to think it would last. The ability to live among them, people who do not deserve to be exposed to someone like me. Broken and filled with hate."

Fergus let out a sigh, shaking his head. "Come along then. Was about to eat me mutton. Once yer belly is filled, ye can clean up the cabin. Tis not fit for living in at the moment."

Although bent over with age, the old man was spry, making quick time to his cabin, which looked in much better shape than the one Duncan planned to live in.

"I will get work and pay rent."

"I know," Fergus replied. "As much as I can use the coin. I hope it will not be for long."

They settled inside the man's humble home and ate the surprisingly good meal. The rest of the day, Duncan worked on the empty cottage's roof. Huge gaping holes in the thatched covering had to be repaired.

That night, he slept on Fergus's floor until a nightmare shook him awake.

He hurried out, at first confused by his surroundings, before realizing where he was. In his mind, the cracks of a whip still sounded again and again, and he pressed the heels of both hands against his ears. It didn't help since the sounds were inside his head.

What sounded like a moan made him whirl toward the

woods where a bed appeared, on it was Beatrice wearing a flowing white gown. Arm stretched, she held out her hand. "Come darling."

"No," Duncan said and moved backward, knowing it wasn't real.

"Duncan." Her voice sounded hollow, sad.

"No," he grunted, turned away, and hung his head. It was not going to be easy, the new memories mixing with the old. Some beautiful and the others terrifying.

By the time he was settled enough to lay back down, it was almost dawn. Daylight helped, but only a little. The tormentors in his head cared little for time.

The next several days passed quickly. He spent the days working and the nights fighting the monsters in his head.

"The roof looks good. Ye are a fast worker," Fergus said craning his neck to get a better look as Duncan slathered mud on the outer walls for better insulation during the winter.

"I am going to the village. Ye said ye wanted some things," Fergus explained motioning to a small wagon with a mule hitched to it.

"A pair of blankets, some whiskey, and a pot," Duncan replied and pulled out his coin sack. He'd already given Fergus more than he'd asked for rent. "Get a new blanket for yerself as well."

The old man grinned, showcasing the gap between his few teeth. "Aye, and a pint or two of ale as well." Climbing to the bench, the man made a tsking sound, and the mule pulled away.

Duncan continued working on the walls, refusing to consider that this would be his home. Instead, he concentrated on each handful of mud. The mixing, the smell of it, and the weight of it in his hands.

Hopefully as time passed, the terrors would lessen. What he wished to never lose, were memories of his wife. Her face, voice, and the sensation of her body against his.

"Beatrice," he said into the wind. "I love ye. I hope ye believed it."

WEEKS LATER, DUNCAN cooked a rabbit, his gaze concentrating on the fire in the hearth. The cottage was finally done, and he was comfortable enough.

He'd kept busy building a table, two chairs, and a bed so he would not have to sleep on the ground. A merchant traveling by had gifted him a mat and some cups for allowing him to sleep there during a rainy night.

It was all he needed. To pass each day, unable to distinguish between them. Other than occasionally speaking to Fergus, who seemed to understand he needed to be alone, he hadn't spoken to another person in many days.

He often wondered what Beatrice did and pictured her in the mornings, hair disheveled, as she chose what to wear that day. He'd loved her expressions, the bottom lip between her teeth, and the way her blue eyes flashed to him when happy or annoyed.

More than anything, he missed making love to her, the sounds she made during and the huskiness of her voice when finding release. The woman enjoyed bedsport. That they'd learned to be lovers together was something he was thankful for.

"Duncan," Fergus called from outside. "I need help."

He rushed out to find Fergus bent over, breathing harshly. "My chest... it hurts..." Fergus stumbled forward, Duncan caught him, and carried the man inside.

"Breathe slowly. Give yerself time to catch yer breath," Duncan said unsure what else he could do to help.

He poured whiskey into a cup and held it up to the man's lips. "Drink."

Taking a sip, Fergus coughed and sputtered when the strong liquid slid down his throat. He grabbed Duncan's tunic tightly. "I am glad not to die alone."

"Ye are not dying," Duncan said attempting to convince himself of it as well. "Ye are just ill."

Fergus shook his head. "It is my heart. I know it." His unfocused gaze pinned Duncan. "Ye must return to her. Make amends. Work on what ails ye, without abandoning yer wife."

"It is for her own good. I cannot subject her to being married to someone like me."

"Would ye wish for her... to leave if she were in yer shoes?"

Duncan swallowed, not wanting to argue with a dying man. "Concentrate on breathing old man."

"Ye love her. Fight for yer marriage."

"Ye do not know how I feel." Duncan couldn't keep the resentment from his voice. "I am not a young lad that cannot control his feelings."

Fergus gasped and grimaced. "I hurt. Give me more whiskey."

Once again Duncan poured the amber liquid into his mouth. "Take yer time."

The man's eyes closed, and Duncan waited to see what

would happen. When Fergus opened them again, it was as if he could not focus. "Fear made me run away. Fear kept me here. Do not be like me."

He coughed and clutched his chest and then Fergus died.

Hours passed and Duncan sat with his back against the wall. Fergus's body remained on the ground where he died. His unseeing eyes staring up to the ceiling.

A humming sound that had echoed in his ears finally ceased and Duncan closed his eyes allowing the silence of the moment to pour over him. It was the first time in many days that his mind was quiet. There was no fear, no sense of impending doom. Only pure silence.

Outside his horse neighed, the sound bringing him to action. Fergus deserved a burial, so Duncan would wrap him and take him to the vicar at the village so he could be laid to rest in the small graveyard.

THE MULE THAT pulled the wagon seeming to understand that someone other than his master drove. The animal looked over his shoulder to Duncan, its sullen eyes taking him in.

"I am sure the vicar will be appreciative of ye and will give ye a good home," Duncan soothed the beast although it didn't understand a word.

His horse made grunting noises, obviously considering it was beneath him to be tethered to a wagon pulled by a mule.

When they arrived at the small vicarage, the man hurried out. "What happened?" He looked to the shrouded body. "Fergus?"

Duncan nodded. "Aye, he died just this morning." He gave no other information, there was no need for it. The man had lived a long life. Before that day, Duncan would have added that Fergus lived a good life. However, it seemed that Fergus hid from whatever he feared. Living alone in a small cottage deep in the woods."

"He was a good man," the vicar said shaking his head. "Helped many a wayward traveler." The man's knowing gaze sized Duncan up. "I am sure ye are aware of that."

"Did he have family?" Duncan asked as he began digging a grave where the vicar pointed.

The man gave Duncan a confused look. "Ye lived with him for a long time, did ye not learn his story?"

Duncan shook his head. "I was unable to hear much in those days."

"One day in a storm, Fergus lost control of the horse that pulled a wagon. The animal, along with his wife and two bairns, plunged into a deep ravine. Fergus and a daughter were thrown from it and survived. He left the girl with family and fled, too grieved with self-blame to remain and raise the wee lass."

It took a long time for Duncan to finish digging the grave. By the time it was done, several villagers gathered to hear the vicar pray over Fergus's body. He was well liked in the village it seemed. One woman even cried, wiping at her eyes as he was lowered into the ground.

Despite what he'd been through, the man had found ways to help others throughout the rest of his life.

As the people dispersed, the vicar stood for a few moments later. "Come inside, join us for a meal before going back."

The vicar's wife was a jolly woman, with rosy cheeks and bright eyes. She wore her hair tucked into a cap that suited her face. "Ye should move here to the village," the woman insisted. "The woods are no place for a young man to live."

It didn't take much to see that she was already plotting to find him a wife.

"I am sure Fergus would like ye to keep the land and continue to help others who travel through," the vicar said between bites. "Although the cottages are old, they are sturdy. Fergus told me that ye fixed the abandoned one."

At the thought that he would die alone like Fergus, without a purpose in life other than waiting for wayward travelers, Duncan's stomach clenched. The entire time the vicar's wife packed a basket of food for him to take, he couldn't keep from thinking the future the vicar had described was not his calling.

"Ye do not have to heat up the meat pie, it will hold for a of couple days," the woman said with a wide smile.

"I appreciate it," he told the vicar's wife as he and her husband walked back out.

The man met his gaze. "Ye should return to yer people. When we run away from our problems, we do not realize that they come with us. Whatever yer troubles are, ye should seek courage from God."

Duncan remained silent, unsure what exactly he would do. "Do ye know of someone who would want to live out there, in Fergus' cottage?"

The vicar thought for a long moment. "There is someone. He is without a home and has been living in a farmer's barn. I will go speak to him."

"Thank ye." Duncan mounted his horse. He would not return to the cottage, but instead headed to the shore to hire a bìrlinn.

CHAPTER EIGHTEEN

ELLA WALKED ALONG the loch's shore and stared off into the distance. Being away from the sea was different. Interesting how very distinct the smell and sound of the loch were in comparison.

Her mother and Lady Macdonald had spent the day sewing a quilt for Isobel to take back with her, while Darach and both Macdonald sons had gone hunting for the day.

Poor Beatrice spent most of the days in her bedchamber. She joined them for some meals, but the rest of the time she spent alone. Her friend was brokenhearted, and Ella wanted nothing more than to find Duncan and drag him back to his wife.

At the same time, she knew her brother's demons must have returned, affecting him so hard that it had forced him to flee.

Caelan sent the letters that Duncan left to both Darach and Beatrice. In the letter to the family, he had apologized for leaving and asked that they forgive him for making the family look bad in the eyes of the Macdonald. He also asked that they not search for him.

Knowing her brothers, Ella was sure both Caelan and Gideon had been dispatched to find him and bring him home.

When she turned to the keep, her brother and the Macdonald men had returned from their hunt. They rode toward the keep, a large boar in a cart behind them.

They would be in good spirits, Ella mused, her gaze focused on Evander Macdonald. He was an attractive man, with golden-brown hair and a handsome face. His broken nose told of his quick temper and his two-colored eyes reminded her of Duncan.

Ella wondered why her mother had not considered one of the Macdonald's as a possible match for her. Her mother had yet to find a suitable husband for her, and Ella was not about to complain. Being she was the only female sibling, her brothers found fault with every suitor that had attempted to court her. At times it was frustrating, but when the suitors were old or ugly, she was glad for it.

A sigh escaped and she shook her head. Evander was not the man for her. He was to be laird one day and it was certain that his marriage would be one arranged by his father.

She considered Padraig, he was handsome and roguish. Already she'd spied three women leaving his bedchamber since arriving. Like her brother Gideon, Padraig would make a good husband one day, but not anytime soon.

Making her way back to the keep, Ella mused on what the day would bring. More time sewing, a delicious meal, and perhaps some time with the family.

The Macdonalds were welcoming people and Ella felt comfortable there. She'd visited several times over the years with her mother and each time, it was a nice break from the routine of life in South Uist.

When she fell sideways, it took a moment to realize her foot had slipped between two rocks. It was only seconds later that agony registered and she cried out. A sharp pain raced from her ankle, up her leg, and Ella could not keep the tears back.

She didn't dare move her foot as every little movement made her cry harder.

One of the riders made his way toward her. Ella squeezed her eyes shut as pain shot up her leg again.

"Do not move," Evander called out as he guided his horse toward where she was.

He dismounted and walked closer to look at her foot and then met her gaze. "I was about to take my horse to the stables when I saw ye fall," he explained. "Yer foot is caught. I will have to move the rocks. It will hurt."

ELLA NODDED, ANGRY that he saw her cry. "I am crying because I'm angry."

His lips curved softening the hard angles of his face. "I would be crying because my ankle was broken."

"D-do ye think it is broken?"

He shrugged and looked up at the sky. "A bird."

Ella followed his line of vision and yelped when he moved a rock and lifted her foot from its trapping.

"There isn't anything nearby to tie to yer foot. I will take ye to the house, the ride will be painful."

"Very well," Ella said fortifying herself for the next movement. "Please help me to stand."

"Put yer arms around my neck," Evander instructed and lifted her up in his arms and although the pain was horrible, the feeling of being in his strong arms took a bit of her attention away from it.

Instead of mounting, he walked toward the keep with her in his arms.

Her ankle protested every movement until she could not help but begin to cry again. "It hurts," she explained while doing her best to keep the tears at bay. "I am sorry to cry on yer tunic."

The brown and hazel gaze met hers. "Cry all ye wish. It may help with the pain."

"Truly?"

"I think so."

When they got to the inner courtyard, Ella had stopped crying. The throbbing intensified with each step Evander took. She let out short pants to keep from screaming while considering that getting the foot cut off would be less painful.

"Goodness, what happened?" Her mother rushed over to them when they entered the house.

Lady Macdonald motioned to a table. "Put her on here."

When lowered, her foot touched the tabletop and Ella let out a scream. To her further embarrassment, Evander hovered over her for a long moment, as if his gaze alone would remove the pain.

In a way, it did distract her. He was very attractive and perhaps she'd not noticed before the cleft in his chin.

"Oh!" she cried out when someone touched her foot. "What are ye doing? Leave it be."

A man, who she assumed was the family healer, gave her an impatient look. His bushy brows furrowed in disapproval. "We must remove the shoe. It will hurt, but it cannot be helped."

"Take my hand," Darach said, replacing Evander at her

side. "Squeeze it as hard as ye need to."

Not only did she squeeze her brother's hand with all her might, but others had to hold her down while the healer set her ankle and splinted it.

At one point the room swirled, and she prayed to pass out; unfortunately, Ella remained conscious the entire time.

Whatever was poured down her throat began to take effect and she welcomed the lack of feeling. The surroundings blurred as someone carried her to the bedchamber and placed her on the bed. Moments later, the wonderful elixir lulled her to sleep.

"ARE YE IN pain?" Beatrice sat in a chair next to the bed, her pretty face drawn with worry. "Mother said it was a horrible break."

Ella shook her head. "I cannot believe what happened. My foot slipped between two rocks and down I went."

Beatrice cringed. "It sounds horrible."

When she moved her leg, the foot hurt, but not enough to warrant more tonic.

"I can call for the healer," Beatrice must have noticed her grimace.

"It does not hurt overmuch," Ella said and studied her friend. "How are ye?"

After releasing a sigh, Beatrice managed a smile. "Better with every day that passes. I still cannot bring myself to forgive Duncan, but I do understand why he left."

Ella huffed. "It is unforgivable to slight yer family in that manner. Darach continues to apologize to yer father for it daily."

"He shouldn't have to." Beatrice turned to the window and then back to Ella's bandaged foot. "Now we will not be able to go for walks together."

The weather was becoming colder, the bitter wind would soon make it hard to spend more than a few minutes outdoors. Ella didn't mention it to Beatrice, instead she shrugged. "We can spend time journaling. I do need to practice my letters so that I can write as neatly as ye."

"I will show ye," Beatrice replied brightening. "Our mothers are making one last trip to the village. I will ask that they purchase two journals and new quills for us."

"A wonderful idea," Ella said and meant it. She'd admired Beatrice's penmanship and was excited at the prospect of improving hers.

BEATRICE WENT DOWN the corridor to find her mother. Hopefully, they'd not left for their weekly trip to the village. The sitting room was empty, so she hurried down the stairs. Upon hearing voices, she went to the dining hall.

Her father, mother, Lady Mariel, and Darach sat around the table talking. Upon her entrance, the conversation ceased, and everyone seemed surprised to see her.

"Did something happen?" Beatrice asked nearing the table.

Darach held what looked to be a letter that he placed his hand over. The discreet movement didn't fool her for one moment.

"Tell me."

Her father motioned to a chair. "It is a message from Stuart about yer husband."

Knees buckling, she lowered to a chair. "Did something happen to Duncan?"

Darach began reading, but after the first few words, Beatrice did not wish to hear anymore. Apparently, Gideon and Ewan had given up trying to find him. They'd found a place that he'd been living at for the last months, but he'd left by the time they arrived.

"The weather is much too cold for them to be out looking for someone who does not wish to be found," Beatrice said meeting Darach's gaze. "Why would ye put yer brothers' lives in danger?"

Lady Mariel placed a hand over Darach's to stop him from replying and spoke. "Because he is my first-born child. They did it for me. Despite doing my best to remain strong, every day I am aggrieved at not knowing his fate." A tear trickled down the woman's face and she wiped it away. "However, Ewan and Gideon are also my sons, and I am relieved they have returned to Keep Ross and will remain there safely for the winter."

The frivolity of asking for journals and quills disappeared and instead Beatrice left the room and walked past the kitchens to the inner courtyard. Once there, it still felt confined. So instead, she hurried up the outdoor stairs until reaching the rooftop.

There were only two guards on duty. One of the guards neared greeting her with a cheery smile. "Miss Beatrice, it is very cold up here. Ye should have worn something heavier if ye plan to remain for long."

She shook her head. "I feel a bit overheated; the cold does

not bother me right now."

Seeming to sense she needed time alone, the men went to the far corner and kept watch. Beatrice wasn't sure why she'd gone there, but the view from there had always calmed her. Perhaps it was why these men seemed in good spirits. In the distance she could see the seashore, the huge expanse that seemed to go to the end of the world.

When she turned to the opposite side, green mountains made for a beautiful background to the village and farms they sheltered.

On the winding road, a wagon pulled by a horse made its way toward the keep. The guards immediately moved to keep watch, tracking its progress. One of them called down to another who then called to the men who guarded the outer courtyard gates.

No longer interested in who the people were that headed toward them, Beatrice decided to go back inside. She closed her eyes and took a deep breath, somehow the news that Duncan remained gone was not bad news. It would have been worse to hear he'd returned home and not to her.

When she opened her eyes, a lone rider appeared. He headed from the seaside in the direction of the keep.

"A rider," Beatrice called over her shoulder to the guards, who hurried to her side.

Whoever he was, he seemed to be in a hurry, urging the horse to gallop at full strides.

The guard once again called down to another, who informed those at the gates of the rider approaching.

Beatrice turned away, it mattered little to her who came and went. If anything, she planned to go to her bedchamber or perhaps Ella's and stay there until whoever it was left.

Then something made her look back. The rider wore Ross colors. The green and black standing out from the usual red and yellow of her clan.

The closer the rider came, the harder her heart thundered in her chest. It was him.

Duncan had come to North Uist.

Beatrice hurried to the stairs, raced down them, and then through the great room. She went up the stairwell to the second floor, to her bedchamber, and slammed the door behind. Her hands trembled as she fought to insert the metal key into the lock, but she managed to lock the door firmly. Once that was complete, she pushed a table in front of it, and not satisfied with that, a chair joined the blockade.

Unable to form a thought, she couldn't keep from rushing to the window to look out. Despite her view of the opposite side, she could glimpse the side of the inner courtyard where visitors had to pass to enter the house.

The guards would stop Duncan, of that, she was sure. He would not be allowed to enter until Evander allowed it.

"Oh no," Beatrice said out loud. Her brothers would not be happy to see her husband. There would be a fight. She had absolutely no doubt about it.

Unhappy with the view, Beatrice struggled to move the furniture and then unlocked the door. Duncan would not come inside directly. Whatever had to happen would take place in the courtyard. She had plenty of time to lock herself in.

At the end of the corridor, she could look over from a balcony to the great hall. The house remained quiet. Then a guard hurried past toward the dining room to alert her father about an approaching rider.

Moments later, Evander and Padraig rushed past and out the front door. Her mother and Lady Mariel came next, pushing her father's rolling chair.

Beatrice stepped back, not wanting to be seen and went to Evander's bedchamber. From his balcony she'd be able to see everything, and hopefully keep from being seen.

Upon Duncan entering the outer courtyard, he dismounted and stable lads came to take his horse. Evander held out a hand shouting for them to stay back. "He will not be staying."

Without a break in his stride, Duncan stalked toward her brothers. He was like a wild man, his hair now past his shoulders, flying in the breeze. There was an intensity about him that if not for her brother's fiery temper should have warned them to maintain a safe distance.

"I must speak to yer father," Duncan called out.

"Ye are not welcome here," Evander shouted back, advancing toward Duncan, Padraig at his side. "Leave."

Beatrice was glad for her bird's eye view. Her parents and Lady Mariel could not see past the gate of the inner courtyard. However, Beatrice was sure they could hear what was said.

"I will not go anywhere until I speak to Laird Macdonald and my wife."

"Ye gave up any rights to make demands upon abandoning my sister," Padraig responded seeming barely able to keep from tackling Duncan to the ground.

A gasp escaped when Duncan rushed her brothers. Catching them by surprise, he was able to make it to the inner gates where he collided with a pair of guards. His size and speed gave him enough momentum to get past them as well. By the time he reached the inner courtyard, Evander and Padriag had caught up with him.

Evander's fist connected with Duncan's jaw first, Padraig managed to hit him in the stomach before Duncan swung and punched her younger brother so hard, he stumbled backward.

With a deep growl Evander charged, and both tumbled to the ground. Duncan got to his feet first and upon Evander standing, he rushed him. The grappling men crashing through the garden fence. A pair of maids screamed and scurried away just as Padraig joined the fight.

Her brothers struggled to gain dominance over Duncan. He was much too large and muscular to contain. First, he lifted Padraig and tossed him into a horse trough, and then he grabbed Evander about the waist and like a heavy stone threw him in the air until her brother landed in the center of the garden patch.

While her brother recovered, Darach appeared. Duncan hesitated when his brother neared.

It was a mistake.

The golden-haired laird swung wide, his fists hitting her husband hard, first in the face and secondly in his midsection. The hits were so powerful, Duncan sailed backward and landed on his back.

Darach stood over him with clenched fists. "Do not dare get up." Like a lion defending against attack, Darach's deep voice seemed to boom.

"Ye have disrespected this place enough, brother."

At this point, Beatrice gave up trying to remain hidden and leaned out to get a clear view of what would happen next.

DUNCAN TRIED TO catch his breath. His brother could always beat him with his hard punches. Although he was stronger, Darach hit harder. Even if Darach had not knocked him to his arse, he would not have hit him back. His brother was also his laird and demanded respect.

The Macdonalds glared down at him, but Duncan kept from looking at them by keeping his attention past Darach's shoulder to Beatrice. She stood on a balcony, her attention locked on what occurred and Duncan was ashamed of losing his temper with her brothers.

"I should not have fought back," he said to Darach and spit out blood.

"Ye should not have come at all," his brother replied. "Get on yer horse and come with me."

Without a word, Darach walked to where Duncan's horse was held by a stable lad. "Ye will not seek to speak to the laird or come here again unless granted permission." Darach glanced to where Beatrice stood.

"By yer actions, I would be very surprised if they grant it."

Duncan mounted and rode out. He didn't dare look to his wife, too afraid to see hatred. Instead, he looked to his mother, who met his gaze and mouthed, "I love ye." With one hand splayed on her chest, she looked about to cry.

In his rashness, he'd ended up making things worse. If the Macdonalds would have considered allowing him to seek an audience with the laird, now they would definitely deny it.

After a few moments, Darach rode out to where he was. Together they continued toward the local village without saying too much.

"How is she?" Duncan asked.

His brother shrugged. "Brokenhearted. Barely leaves her bedchamber. As one would expect a wife to be after her husband insults her family and leaves her."

"I did not want to do it."

Darach met his gaze. "We understand ye, Duncan. I know what all ye have been through. However, that does not excuse what ye did."

"Seeing him. Farlan. It brought it all back. I have spent the last weeks unable to push past it. I was not in any shape to face her family; it took all my willpower to remain after that day in the forest."

His brother was silent. It didn't bode well that Darach had no advice to give. It was as if a heavy boulder rested on his shoulders and Duncan could not sit straight. "I should return home or perhaps leave Uist altogether."

"Ye will stay here in the village. I will present yer case to the Macdonald. If ye wish me to give Beatrice a message, I can do that as well. Once a decision is reached, one way or another, I will come to inform ye."

"When are ye returning home?" Duncan asked at a loss for what else should be said.

"Winter has been mild, Mother had decided to return when we got the message that Ewan and Gideon could not find ye. I am not sure now. Perhaps another fortnight."

When they reached the village tavern, the brothers dismounted. Over a tankard of ale, Darach told him what happened to Ella. "She may have to remain behind until the spring. The break was quite extensive."

After finishing his drink, Darach met his gaze. "Do ye have coin to pay for lodging?"

Duncan nodded. "I do."

Motioning to the serving woman, Duncan ordered a bowl of food and another tankard of ale. He wondered how long it would be before word came.

"Tell her I love her," he said, then shook his head. "No. Forget it."

"What about Evander and Padraig?" Darach asked.

"I am sorry."

CHAPTER NINETEEN

"**B**EATRICE, OPEN THE door," her mother's voice rose with annoyance. "Now."

On heavy feet, she went to the door and unlocked it. "I am not in a good frame of mind today. I am not sure I want to talk about what happened."

"How ye feel about what just occurred is very important. Yer father wishes for us to gather to discuss what to do."

"Should we not wait until the Ross returns?"

"He just did," her mother replied motioning to the door. "Let us go."

It had been a long time since Beatrice had cared about her appearance. She'd only worn the serviceable dresses that allowed for going outdoors and helping in the garden or feeding the goats. She'd not cared about her more elaborate gowns that suddenly felt silly and something someone without a care in the world would don.

Interesting how much things changed in a matter of weeks.

Upon entering the parlor, everyone was already seated. Evander turned to her, his left eye purpling from the fight. She looked to Padraig. He had a swollen bottom lip and a cut above his right eye.

Her father cleared his throat and directed his comment to Darach. Most of the conversation would be between the lairds, with words from the rest only when requested.

"Yer brother seems to hold little regard for the rules of our people. He offended me and my clan by ignoring my invitation. Even worse, he hurt my daughter. I have no tolerance for a man who abandons his wife." At the stern words, Beatrice's chest and stomach clenched. What could Darach say that could possibly change her father's mind about Duncan.

The Ross looked first to Lady Mariel, who gave a soft nod. Whatever he was about to say, he'd sought her council first.

"My brother is a kind, brave, and proud man. However, he is also a broken and damaged man, who has yet to overcome his past." Darach met Beatrice's gaze. "I am not sure if he divulged to ye the cause of each of his scars."

Turning back to her father, he continued. "There is very little of my brother's body that is not scarred from whippings, broken bones, and other forms of torture that his captors imposed on him during the years of his captivity. Duncan spent days, sometimes weeks without food and water and then was forced to fight against able-bodied men for a piece of moldy bread. When they wished to kill captives, it was Duncan who was told how to do it. If he refused, then he and the other prisoner would be whipped until he did it. My brother often prayed for a death that did not come while left in the dark, rats feasting on his bloodied body. This repeated itself for ten long years. When Duncan became terribly ill, the others on the ship were afraid to catch whatever he had. They threw him overboard. Feverish and malnourished, it was a miracle he survived. That is how he was able to return to us."

Lady Mariel wiped at a tear, doing her best not to cry harder. Beatrice blinked away tears at learning even more than she already knew about her husband's horrible past.

"I tell ye this, not for ye to forgive my brother's transgressions, but for ye to understand why he left recently." Darach cleared his throat, overcome with emotion. "Just a few days before we came here, my brother was trapped by a man from one of the ships he'd been held at. The man hung Duncan upside down and stabbed him several times, planning to let him bleed to death. It would have happened if not for Stuart and Gideon arriving just in time."

"My goodness," Beatrice's mother exclaimed and then took Lady Mariel's hand. "I am so sorry."

"After this current experience, Duncan was not well," Darach let out a sigh. "I am not sure why he left, but I presume to rid the plague in his head."

The room was silent for a long beat while her father digested the information.

Beatrice was not aware of the horrors Duncan had been through. Her heart broke for the young man, who'd been torn from his family and home and subjected to such heartbreaking treatment for so long.

"What did he ask ye to tell me?" her father asked.

"He asks for a second opportunity to meet with ye and wishes to make amends with the clan and to regain Beatrice's trust."

Everyone waited as the lairds continued speaking. Beatrice was not sure she was ready to talk to Duncan. Despite everything, she was hurt. He had abandoned and humiliated her by being forced to return home without him.

Now he returned from wherever he'd gone, prepared to make amends. What exactly did that mean? That she should immediately forgive and forget?

"I will meet with Duncan," her father said and then studied her for a moment. "It will be up to Beatrice if she wishes to speak to him. He broke trust with my daughter and that is not something easy to recover from."

When Darach turned to her, Beatrice did not meet his gaze. It was impossible to know what she'd feel in the next hours, but in that moment, she could not fathom speaking to him. All she did was shake her head.

"I will go see him, and inform him of yer decision," Darach told her father.

Beatrice hurried from the room to seek the solace of her bedchamber. A part of her was relieved to know that Duncan was alive and well. The larger portion of her was too angry and hurt to consider a simple discussion with him.

"Did ye know what had happened to yer husband?" Isobel strolled in and immediately sat on the bed next to her. "My heart breaks for him."

"I knew a bit. Although I am sure there are still many things Darach did not tell. From the scars on Duncan's body, I can tell he went through some horrific times."

"Ye are not ready to forgive him are ye?" Isobel asked, her dark eyes searching her face. "I understand. I am not sure I could either if I were in yer place."

"I love him," Beatrice blurted. "With all my heart. And he professed to feel the same. How could he leave, not try to be with me and allow us to work together against the demons in his head?" Beatrice slammed her fist into the soft bedding. "I am so very angry with him."

Isobel let out a long sigh. "Ye know that in the end ye will return to him and over time forgive what he did. I strongly suggest ye take all the time needed. If it is a season or even a year before ye return, then so be it."

Her sister was right. There were no limitations to how long she could take to decide.

She let out a long sigh and leaned her head on Isobel's shoulder. "I am so very thankful for ye and my family."

"I do think ye should return with us. To Keep Ross of course."

THE HOUSE WAS silent as Duncan walked through the great room towards the stairwell. Upon reaching the second floor, the new chambermaid Beatrice had hired walked out of Beatrice's bedchamber and jumped at noticing him.

"Dear me," she exclaimed. "I apologize Mister Duncan, ye startled me."

He gave a nod. "No need. I know I have been gone a long time."

The woman studied him for a moment as if assessing if she could trust him. She then crouched down and picked up a cloth she'd dropped.

"When will Lady Beatrice return?" The question was innocent enough, but it speared Duncan through the heart.

"I am not sure as yet," he replied and continued toward his bedchamber. Once he washed up and changed, he had to speak with Caelan and learn how things had continued with the livestock his brother was breeding.

He was pleasantly surprised to note all seemed to be in

order, the grounds kept up and the house orderly. Of course, Caelan would have it no other way.

His brother would have questions that he was not up to answering, but he owed him that much.

While washing up, he thought of the conversation with Laird Macdonald. While Beatrice's father had remained curt and distant, he was not unreasonable. He'd informed Duncan that he should return once things between him and Beatrice were resolved. He'd given her the choice of speaking to him and she'd refused.

Whether she came back to South Uist or remained on the northern isle, the Macdonald insisted that Duncan would visit once a season. He'd given his word to do so and then made the trek back home alone.

The bitter cold had cut through his body during the sail back, but he'd welcomed the distraction from the painful realization of possibly losing his incredible wife forever.

Through the window past his half-built wall, Duncan saw Caelan appear on horseback. Wearing a long coat and thick scarf instead of a plaid, he was a picture of a cultured gentleman. An Englishman.

One would think his brother did not fit in the highlands, not with his refined speech and impeccable attention to his appearance. Perhaps because of the way he presented himself, men underestimated his brother. Caelan was a merciless warrior, who fought not to defeat but to kill.

If there was something that his half-brother had inherited from their father, it was brutality. For the most part Caelan kept control, he was keen like a fox and able to get out of menacing situations. However, if a certain line was crossed, there would be hell to pay.

At that moment, he seemed pensive, his gaze locked on the stables. He must have noticed Duncan's horse because he turned his head toward the house next. Although Duncan was sure Caelan could not see him from that distance, it seemed as if he could. Despite this, Calen did not alter his horse's pace or allow the animal to meander.

THE BEDCHAMBER WAS cold, but Duncan did not bother to light the fire. There was wood in the hearth, ready to be lit which meant the lad Beatrice had insisted on hiring ensured that nothing lacked. Water was in the pitcher for washing and fresh cloths hung from the stand.

As if conjured by his thoughts, there was a soft knock and after Duncan called for whoever it was to enter, the young man poked his head in.

"Sir, do ye require me to start the fire? I apologize for my tardiness. I was not aware of yer arrival until just now." The lad was lanky, long-legged with a mop of curly hair and dark brown eyes.

"What is yer name?" Duncan asked, not recalling if he'd ever learned it.

"Ivan, sir."

"Thank ye Ivan, I do not require a fire right now, but would like one after last meal."

"Very well sir." The lad gave him a curt nod and walked back out.

When Duncan returned to the first level, Caelan stood in front of the large hearth warming his hands. He'd removed his coat and thrown it over a chair. More accurately, he'd folded it and then draped it carefully over the back of a chair.

"I did not expect yer return so soon," Caelan said without looking at him. "Are ye well?"

How to answer the question he wasn't sure about? A part of him wished to be back in the forest in the lonely cottage. Rather than to be without Beatrice. At least there he had the excuse of her not knowing where he was.

"Ye take a long time to reply," Caelan's gaze roamed over his body. "Ye seem healthy enough."

Duncan went to a sideboard and lifted a decanter of whiskey and looked to Caelan who nodded. Once he'd poured the liquor into two glasses, he held one out to Caelan. After spending so many days on horseback, he preferred not to sit, so Duncan leaned an elbow on the back of a winged chair. "I went to North Uist. As ye may suspect, I did not receive a warm reception. Laird Macdonald did speak to me after two days, which I spent in the village."

"And yer wife?"

"She refused," Duncan said and swallowed another mouthful of whiskey. "I do not blame her."

The aroma of roasting meat wafted from the kitchen and Duncan inhaled it, filling his lungs with the enticing smell. Food was the great comforter, freely shared when people gathered for unpleasant things like burials and was brought to the sickly to make them feel better.

"I have no doubt Beatrice will return. She loves ye."

Duncan stared into his empty glass. "I humiliated her. That she had to face her family alone so soon after marrying was cruel. I am not sure she should forgive me."

"There are some people attempting to settle southeast of

here, on the other side of the forest. I saw them today but did not approach. Seem to be men, who'd pulled ashore. About twenty, I decided it was best to alert Stuart."

"We should go now."

"I sent two guardsmen to Keep Ross late this morning, and two are keeping watch not too far from the camp to ensure we are not encroached upon. Once we eat, we can take their place and allow them to come here to eat and rest. I assume the guardsmen from the keep will arrive shortly."

THEY SPENT THE night keeping watch. The men who camped looked to be warriors. They were well armed, but it wasn't clear what clan they belonged to as they wore no colors and flew no banners. Currently, they spoke in low tones while roasting whatever they'd caught over a small fire. It was a frigid night. The small fire would do little to keep them warm.

Because of them camping on the eastern shore, Duncan assumed they'd have to have traveled from either Skye or Eriskay. That meant they could be Maclean. If clan Maclean, it would mean trouble. Clan Maclean from Skye were enemies of both them and the MacNeil.

The thundering of hooves alerted not only Caelan and Duncan of the approach of a huge army, but also the men who'd set up camp. They scrambled to arm themselves and waited with tense stances for whoever appeared.

Stuart had not held back. Flank after flank of horsemen rode in from the shore and through the forest. Stuart, with his huge bow strapped to his back, rode forward, flanked by Gideon and Ewan, all of whom wore the Ross clan tartan of green and black.

Eager to join their brothers, both he and Caelan had already mounted and rode to the front to see what happened.

The men on the ground stood in a large circle. They were outmanned but did what they could to defend themselves. Horsemen blocked their access to the birlinns they'd come in on. They were surrounded.

"We seek an audience with Laird Ross to ask for asylum," a large muscled, heavily bearded man spoke out. "We fled for our lives."

Stuart looked over to Duncan. As the eldest one present, he had the last word. However, the men before them did not have to know that. He gave his brother a slight nod, letting him know to make the decision.

"What clan do ye claim?"

The muscled man looked to his men. "Maclean, but no longer." He then continued, "I am called Lennox."

"Build a larger fire to keep warm. Ye and yer men will be escorted to another place in the morning. My men will remain," Stuart said. He then ordered the guardsmen to remain and keep the newcomers from leaving.

INSTEAD OF RETURNING to the keep, all four brothers rode to the house with a large contingency of guardsmen.

Half of the men would sleep inside the house on the floor of the great room and parlor. Another twenty or so would crowd into the stables. A few would sleep in the guardroom and storehouse.

Somehow a place was found for everyone.

The four brothers went upstairs to the sitting room as every other room downstairs was taken. Gara and Firtha, along with the new chambermaid rushed to and fro, immediately heating fermented cider to warm the cold men.

Knowing it was fruitless to try to stop the eager women, neither Duncan nor Caelan tried to talk them out of it.

Within moments of sitting, the young lad, Ivan, entered with cups of the hot cider for them as well.

"I am glad to see ye have returned," Stuart said, and then kept silent. He was the type of man, who waited to be informed of things—unless it was urgent. His hazel gaze roamed over the faces of the others and he raked a hand through his dark shoulder length hair. "I am not sure what to think about them. They could be here as spies for the Maclean."

"Aye, that was my first thought," Caelan said.

Gideon nodded. "One of us should return to the keep. To ensure none of them snuck through." He frowned at Duncan. "When did ye get back?"

Ewan, who was almost identical in looks to Stuart stood. "Perhaps Gideon is right. I will ride back to the keep and ensure all is well." He put his cup down. "I will ensure the keep is well secured until ye arrive in the morning." After a long look at Duncan, he lifted an eyebrow. "Ye look as if ye've been dragged behind yer horse."

CHAPTER TWENTY

S TUART LAY ON a pallet in front of the fireplace in Duncan's bedchamber. Gideon was in the bedchamber across the corridor, usually used by their mother. No one wanted to sleep in Beatrice's.

"Why did ye not wish to reply today when the man asked to speak to our laird?" Stuart asked looking up at the ceiling.

If anyone would make an exceptional laird, it was Stuart. He had an even temperament and was a fair man; he thought decisions through. Feeling better suited for battle than leading, Duncan preferred that his brother cede lairdship duties to Stuart or Caelan over him.

"I have never aspired to be laird, nor leader other than perhaps with warriors. Even then, sometimes my judgment is clouded by my past. I do not trust it."

The silence that stretched indicated Stuart was measuring his words. "Each of us has their own strengths. It is good for a man to recognize his strengths and limitations."

Despite the hole in his chest left from Beatrice's absence, Duncan chuckled at his carefully phrased reply.

THE NEXT MORNING went without anything of alarm to note. As planned, they escorted the Maclean's to where they could keep an eye on them. They were to be housed in the abandoned building that Duncan and Beatrice had sought shelter in. With the bitter cold and being disarmed, the men posed little threat.

"It would have been better if we could leave guards behind, but I am trusting that the weather will prevent them from doing too much harm," Stuart said as they overlooked the settling of the asylum seekers.

Men arrived from the nearby village with blankets and basic food that would hold the men for several weeks.

Lennox, the muscular man who'd been appointed spokesperson came to where Duncan and Stuart stood. "My men and I have pooled our coins and would like to pay for the items ye brought."

"Keep it," Stuart replied. "Ye will need it to purchase more provisions. My brother, Darach, Laird Ross, will be returning and when he does, we will send word for ye to come and speak to him."

The man nodded. "Ye have been most kind."

"I am sure ye will be asked to repay in some way. For now, remain here. There are tools and other items that ye and yer men can use to make repairs to the structure. Ye can cut down trees for firewood or to build whatever ye need, no more."

"May we snare rabbits?" the man asked.

"Aye," Stuart replied. "But nothing else."

With nothing else to be done, they mounted and began the trek to the keep. Duncan had decided to continue with his brothers hoping to get meat pies from Greer. Caelan returned to the house with an additional ten guards that would ride out to patrol the house where the Maclean's settled.

Gideon had remained back at the abandoned building with

fifty men to see about settling the newcomers and ensuring all was well. They would return once Gideon decided all was as well as it could be expected.

UPON NEARING DÚN Láidir, the proud gray stone structure never ceased to catch Duncan by surprise. It was a huge keep that could easily house the entire village within its walls if ever they were under siege.

Atop the walls and top of the main house, men draped in thick capes kept watch, their sharp gazes set in every direction.

The gates were closed, a precaution to the newcomers. They would remain closed for the winter. A bit of an annoyance, but it was necessary to ensure the safety of the family.

"Ewan and Catriona and their bairns have moved in for the rest of winter," Gideon said.

"Why?" Duncan asked.

"Apparently Mother had insisted on it."

A guard rode toward them, the man slowing his horse so he could speak to them.

"The laird and the others have returned."

The news caught Duncan off guard. He looked past the man to the keep gates.

Sensing what he wanted to know, Stuart asked, "Who came back with him?"

"Ladies Mariel, Isobel, and Beatrice."

Stuart turned to Duncan. "Ella must not be well enough to travel. There must be a reason why the visit was cut short. Hopefully it is not bad."

The brothers dismounted as soon as they reached the courtyard and hurried into the house. They walked into a flurry of activity.

Trunks were being carried to bedchambers as their mother directed. Isobel spoke to maids, while Darach spoke to several men.

Next to the hearth in chairs, Catriona sat with a swaddled baby in her lap, the other bairn toddled across the floor toward Beatrice, who held her arms out.

It was the first time he'd seen her in a long time. Her golden hair was pulled away from her face into a long braid. Lips curved into a wide smile as she encouraged the child to walk. When the child took a step, the antics brightened her beautiful face.

"We must speak to Darach," Stuart said. "Report what happened."

"I am sure he has been informed," Duncan replied unable to tear his eyes from his wife. There was something different about her. It was as if she'd blossomed. He couldn't quite figure out what it was. She seemed more serene in a way."

Seeming to sense his regard Beatrice looked up, her clear blue gaze clashing with his. Duncan did not dare close the distance between them. Instead, he gave a nod of greeting. Her eyes narrowed in thought, then she turned her attention back to the bairn.

"There must be something afoot that ye felt the need to gather so many guardsmen," Darach said as he neared. "We must speak."

They went to Darach's study where Stuart filled Darach in on what happened. Their eldest brother taking in every word, nodding occasionally.

"I agree with what ye did. I do not fully trust their purpose for being here, but since it's winter, they will have to remain put for the time being. We will have to alert the men on the southeast coast to keep an eye out for others. If more come, they are to be sent away."

Unable to keep his curiosity at bay any longer, Duncan had to find out why they'd returned sooner. "I thought ye planned to spend the season in North Uist?"

"We did," Darach replied. "However, with the weather remaining relatively mild. I wished to return. Also, Mother missed her grandchildren."

"The Macdonald insisted that Beatrice return with us," Darach said, pinning Duncan with a sharp look.

"Ye should speak to yer wife, do what ye can to reconcile."

CHAPTER TWENTY-ONE

B EATRICE'S HANDS SHOOK and her breathing hitched upon
seeing Duncan. With windblown hair and a thicker
beard, he looked like a savage. A breathtakingly handsome
wild man, who'd not been tamed.

It hurt that he'd not insisted on talking to her, that instead,
he'd turned away and gone with the laird. Then again, she
supposed he was supposed to do what his brother asked.

"Where are my things?" she asked Orla, who hurried
through the great room.

The maid motioned to the stairs. "The same room that ye
and Mister Duncan shared before. I am fetching water so ye
can bathe."

"Thank ye, Orla." Beatrice hurried up the stairs. The corridor was dimly lit as she made her way to the bedchamber. Her
feet felt heavier with each step at recalling the last time they'd
stayed there and how loudly they'd made love.

Just as she passed through the doorway, strong arms
wrapped around her body. Her breath caught upon realizing it
was Duncan. Leaning against his chest, she didn't try to fight
instead waited limply for what he'd do or say next.

Duncan turned her around so that she faced him and once
again pulled her into a hard embrace.

"Forgive me. Forgive me," he murmured over and over, a

catch in his voice. "Please, Beatrice."

The way their bodies fit together soothed the exhaustion. If it was possible, her love for Duncan had grown with each passing day. At the same time, Beatrice could not shake the ache of his leaving.

Pushing away from him, she looked up at him, fighting the urge to sweep the dark hair from his brow. "I have forgiven ye."

"But ye remain hurt."

"When ye did not show up on the day we departed, my heart broke Duncan. It was days before the letter came." Beatrice closed her eyes. "Ye could have talked to me. We could have waited to go had I known how ye felt."

He nodded, the bi-colored gaze not leaving her face. "The realization of what I did finally sunk in and when it did, I almost did not return. I broke yer trust in me, and for that, I cannot forgive myself."

He waited and when she remained silent, he spoke again. "No blame would fall upon ye for not accepting me back as yer husband. It is me that broke our vows and any relationship that was building between us."

"I need to bathe and rest. Can we talk later? My mind is awhirl, I cannot seem to get a straight thought." Beatrice turned to the tub, steam rose from the hot water and she could not wait to sink into it.

The door closed behind her and she let out a long breath. What was she to do? A part of her wanted to be back in North Uist with her family, and not having to worry about the pressure of marriage and forgiveness. As much as she loved and wanted her husband, the fear that he'd leave her over and over made Beatrice hesitate to return to him.

Beatrice sunk into the hot perfumed water that was the perfect antidote for not just her weary body, but also her mind.

The picture of Duncan's face floated in her mind. How could she not remain with the man? He deserved love and patience, but was she strong enough?

There was a light knock and Isobel's face appeared from behind the door. "I came to check on ye. I saw Duncan go down the stairs and outside."

"Outside?"

"Aye, he is over by the vegetable garden, looking forlorn." Isobel lifted a large cloth so that Beatrice could dry herself. The water had cooled quickly, and she disliked cool baths.

"My husband will have to learn that he cannot simply appear and expect to be welcomed back with open arms."

Isobel went to the window and peered out. "Aye, I agree. How I would react if in yer shoes is not an easy answer."

"Ye forgave Darach when he went to see that woman instead of coming straight home upon his release from imprisonment."

For a split second, Beatrice wondered if she'd been unthoughtful in her comment, but Isobel shrugged it away. "I was very angry at him. It seems ye are in a similar situation. Having to decide whether to trust yer husband or not. If the answer is no, then ye should return to our parent's home."

Our parent's home. No longer their home. After marriage wherever their husband was home.

She dressed in a light dress and then donned a thick shawl over her shoulders. "I am not sure how to proceed. I do love him dearly. I will obey my vows and remain with him.

However, I must decide what the terms will be. Overall, I must protect my heart."

"Sit down and talk to him. Come to an agreement that if he finds himself in a similar place in the future, he comes to ye first."

It was much later that she finally sent Orla to find Duncan. She sat in a chair in the bedchamber, in front of the fireplace. The cheery fire did little to calm her nerves. What would Duncan say when she told him her decision? It was very possible, he would walk out of her life forever. It could come to pass that as soon as the weather permitted, she would be back in North Uist without a husband to call her own.

When he entered the room, she let out a steadying breath.

Duncan's gaze studied her and then he lowered into the chair opposite hers.

"Where did ye go?" Beatrice asked, mainly because she was curious.

After a pause, he replied, "To a cabin where I had lived when I first was freed. An old man cared for me and allowed me to live there for many months. As payment, I did work for him. He died while I was there this time."

"Why did ye not think to tell me ye were so troubled?"

"I was fearful of yer reaction to seeing me in a crazed state. The idea that ye would possibly be in danger was worse than knowing I was hurting ye by leaving. Now, I realize that perhaps if I would have shared with ye, it would have helped."

Her heart broke for him and once again grief for his stolen years enveloped her. Of course, he didn't know how to share his emotions or how to properly deal with them. He'd had to face hardships and emotional times alone for so long.

"Duncan, if we are to remain together, I have demands. If ye cannot agree to them, then I will return to North Uist, alone."

There was cautious hope in his expression. "Tell me."

"If I return to the estate, ye and I will share the same bed-chamber. We will have a chapel built for our own personal time of prayer and solace. Lastly, ye will promise to speak to me about how ye feel regularly and are not to become cross when I ask ye about it."

His brows drew together. "I agree to yer demands. They are reasonable and ye are kinder than I deserve."

"Stop saying things like that. Ye are not less deserving than anyone else. I cannot imagine what ye have been through. I am sure others who have gone through the same have ended up mad or unable to survive with the shadows of the past in their mind."

"Can I stay here with ye tonight?"

Beatrice's lips curved. He looked so forlorn. Her huge beastly husband was so vulnerable in that moment.

"Aye, of course."

"Duncan?"

His gaze met hers waiting for what she'd say.

"Would ye kiss me please? I have missed ye so much."

In an instant, he closed the distance and pulled her up and into his arms. Their mouths collided. There was no feeling like being in Duncan's embrace. The familiar taste and smell of him overtaking her senses with so much force, it was as if being wrapped in warm comforting blankets.

Beatrice raked her fingers down his wide back, as she kissed him back with all her might. Then she slipped her hands under his tunic, running her palms up the uneven skin. Despite the scarring, he was warm and soft.

A gasp escaped at the caresses of the one area no one had ever touched in such a way and he responded by tugging her dress from her shoulders and pushing it down until it flowed to the floor.

Not to be outdone, Beatrice yanked his belt free and pulled the rough fabric of his tunic up. Duncan helped her by pulling it up over his head and dropping it down next to the dress. The breeches and boots followed, and both stood before one another completely undressed.

"Ye are beautiful," Duncan said and moved closer.

When he lowered her onto the bed, she took him in. Duncan was a sight to behold, fully aroused and although a bit thinner still quite magnificent.

"Come to me," she said, arms outstretched. "Show me how ye feel."

The weight of his body over hers was perfect. Once again, they kissed, Beatrice threading her fingers through his hair. The calloused palms brought shivers of awareness as he slid them over every curve before cupping one breast and then the other.

Duncan's uneven breathing made her own hitch. "I want ye so much," he whispered in her ear. "I cannot wait."

When he pushed her legs apart, cool air hit her moist sex and Beatrice gasped at how much desire burned in her. "Take me."

Once settled between her legs, Duncan took himself in hand and guided himself to her entrance. The first nudge sent trails of heat up and down each leg. He pushed in, slowly, taking his time and allowing for adjustment to his girth.

Finally, fully seated, he pulled back out just enough for her to grab his bottom and pull. He drove in and once again filled her completely. Over and over, he slid in and out with measured slowness, driving her to madness.

When she could not stand it any longer and lifted her hips from the bed, Duncan increased his pace.

His hand slid under her hips and he lifted Beatrice off the bed to allow deeper access.

With each thrust and withdrawal, it sent them higher and further into a passionate release. Despite doing her best to remain in the moment Beatrice was spiraling and soon began to cry out as he drove fast and deeper until she lost all control.

Duncan's deep grunts continued, past the point of awareness other than seeking release. His thrusts became swift. Too lost in her own passion, Beatrice couldn't garner any energy to do more than lay under him.

When his mouth covered her breast and he took the tip in, sucking it hard, she cried out a second release threatening.

"Finish with me," Duncan gasped, taking the other tip in, and pulling it with his teeth. It wasn't gentle, but not painful either. There was an effect from his actions. Beatrice began to flail beneath him until she lost grasp of reality, floating above them, free as a bird.

Ten days later...

BEATRICE HURRIED THROUGH the great room to the kitchen in search of Gara. The woman looked up from the pot she stirred when Beatrice entered. "What can I do for ye, Lady Beatrice?"

"I am most hungry this morning," she explained. "Could I have toast and tea? Once Misters Duncan and Caelan rise then we will have first meal together."

The woman gave her a warm look. "Ye have been very hungry since arriving. Are ye with child?"

The thought of it terrified her. Not the having children, those she badly wanted. It was the entire idea of birthing, not something she planned to go through anytime soon. "I certainly hope not," she replied and then amended by stating. "Not so soon anyway."

Gara nodded. "It is a beautiful experience, except for one day." She laughed at her own joke and grinned. "Tea and toast will be brought shortly."

Once seated in the great room, Beatrice considered the possibility of being with child. Unable to remember when her last monthly courses had been, she stood and paced the room. Surely, she must have had them since marrying. In her mind, she calculated the time since her courses had come and left and then began counting days until marrying Duncan.

"Oh no," she whispered harshly.

"Is something wrong?" Duncan had entered and stood near the end of the table.

"I forgot yer mother and Isobel were coming tomorrow. I am not sure to have proper items for a good meal. I will have to travel to the village this morning." It was true, however, that was not the reason she'd uttered the two words.

BY THE END of the day, Beatrice could barely stand keeping it to herself. There was no question, she was with child. Her mind swirled with astonishment and she giggled wondering what Duncan's response would be. She wanted to inform Isobel and Lady Mariel the following day, so it was time to divulge the information to her husband.

When she slipped into the bed, he joined her and turning to his side, kissed her soundly. "I love ye in my bed every night."

"Truth be told," Beatrice replied. "This is my bed."

"We could have remained in my bedroom. There is nothing wrong with it." He nuzzled her neck. "Ye smell so good," the husky murmurs sent shivers of awareness through her.

Beatrice brushed hair from his face and looked at him. "There is something ye have to know."

"What is it?" Immediately he was tense, expecting bad news.

Lips curving, Beatrice teased him, "I think it is good, but ye will have to tell me what ye think. Ye and I will be parents by late spring."

The room went absolutely silent, only the sound of the wood cracking in the fire. It was as if the air left.

Duncan lowered his head and buried his face into her shoulder.

"What is it darling? Are ye crying?" Beatrice lifted his face and looked at his wet cheeks. "I love ye so much."

"I love ye," Duncan replied and once again hid his face. "Thank ye for making me a full man. Bringing happiness to my life."

Overwhelmed with love for him, Beatrice wrapped her arms around him and let out a shaky breath.

"Ye make me happy as well."

When he exhaled fully, Beatrice realized it was the first

time he was so relaxed in her presence. Duncan let go of whatever held him back, his body going limp in surrender.

The healing power of love had begun its work.

Early Spring 1602

STUART'S STEED PRANCED as he rode toward where the Maclean men were housed.

"Stop it," Stuart said to the horse who paid him no heed. He gritted his teeth, the animal seemed to be in some sort of mood. "War horses do not prance," Stuart muttered.

A chuckle came from somewhere between the trees. Whoever it was must have overheard him.

"Who is there?" Stuart said with a firm a voice as he could muster without scaring whoever it was away.

"It is I Mister Stuart," A willowy young woman appeared. She wore the distinct clothing of someone of little means. A drab, but very clean dress, over it a tidy apron. Her hair was covered with a kerchief, pulling her hair back from her pretty face.

"I apologize. I overheard ye scolding yer horse," she said, her wide eyes meeting his. Her eyes were a light brown, framed with long lashes.

"Cait."

She was familiar to him; he'd seen her about the keep lately. "What are ye doing so far from the keep?"

Cait blinked and swallowed nervously. "I am snaring rabbits for my mother and younger brother. I have the Laird's permission," she quickly added, holding up a dead hare.

Untying his bow from the saddle, he then pulled an arrow from the quiver. Cait paled, her eyes not leaving his face.

Pulling back, he released the arrow into nearby bushes. "Now ye have two."

"Thank ye," she stuttered turning to where he'd shot.

Stuart nodded. "Be with care, Cait."

He urged his horse forward but couldn't help looking over his shoulder to see what the woman did.

Cait remained standing and lifted a hand in farewell.

Interesting that he'd never noticed before how beautiful she was.

The saga continues with Stuart and Cait's story, *The Eagle*.

About the Author

Enticing. Engaging. Romance.

USA Today Bestselling Author Hildie McQueen writes strong brooding alphas who meet their match in feisty brave heroines. If you like stories with a mixture of passion, drama, and humor, you will love Hildie's storytelling where love wins every single time!

A fan of all things pink, Paris, and four-legged creatures, Hildie resides in eastern Georgia, USA, with her super-hero husband Kurt and three little yappy dogs.

Join my reader group on Facebook: bit.ly/31YCee1
Sign up for my newsletter and get a free book! goo.gl/jLzPTA
Visit her website at www.hildiemcqueen.com
Facebook: facebook.com/HildieMcQueen
Twitter: twitter.com/authorhildie
Instagram instagram.com/hildiemcqueenwriter

Made in the USA
Coppell, TX
29 October 2021